I0565123

CHRISTINE CHIANTI

SLEEPY HOLLOW HIGH
BOOK 2

WICKED

WINTER

Golden Lark Publishing

Wicked Winter

Published by Golden Lark Publishing

Copyright © 2013 by Robin DeMarco Enterprises, Inc.

Cover image © 2013 by Rora Linn Images

Excerpt from Savage Spring © 2013 Robin DeMarco Enterprises, Inc.

The names Sonex and Aerovee are trademarks of Sonex Aircraft, LLC and are used with permission. More information about these products may be found at

www.sonexaircraft.com

Golden Lark Publishing is a division of

Robin DeMarco Enterprises, Inc.

Golden Lark Publishing

P.O. Box 1602

Lockport, New York 14095-1602

www.goldenlarkpublishing.com

CHAPTER 1

THE SHORTEST DAY

Shivering in the early morning temperatures, I pulled the comforter on my bed up higher and snuggled down. My cocker spaniel, Misty, was sprawled out and pushed into my back. Reality sunk in quickly, and I sat upright with a start. Today was it. The Winter Solstice, and I had made it.

This wouldn't be the typical reaction for a seventeen-year-old high school senior, but I'm not exactly what you would call typical in any sense of things.

My name is Stevie Nixon, and I am a senior this year at Sleepy Hollow High, in Sleepy Hollow, New York. This alone doesn't cause my pedigree to stand out. However, over the past three months, I've discovered that the legend of Sleepy Hollow, including the Headless Horseman and Ichabod Crane, was entirely true.

More to the point, I discovered that my great-times-eight grandfather was the Horseman. It has also come to my attention that, he wasn't exactly a nice guy. In fact, it is highly likely that he killed Ichabod.

Now, here we are, eleven generations later, and I'm facing the fallout. The curse that was placed on my family generations before I was born was thrust into my lap this past September. So, here I am, facing a senior year of trying to find what my distant relative did, whom he hurt and how I can correct things.

From what I learned on the first contact about the curse, I would be given three separate clues, one at each of the change of season, and I would have the season to work out the clue and find a way to complete the task that is embedded.

If I fail at any one of the tasks, I die. That simple.

Yesterday I managed to complete the first task with literally an hour to spare, so to see the breaking day was something that I would never take for granted again.

I tried to bolster my courage. While it may seem like a small distraction, facing a two-hundred-plus year old curse takes a lot out of you. I glanced around the room, almost afraid to see the inevitable thin black box that would contain the next clue and begin what was surely going to be a wicked winter. Regardless of how it turned out, the time between now and the Spring Solstice was going to be interesting.

As I rolled out of the bed, I heard something fall. Turning I picked up the small thin black box that now lay on the floor. I set it on the table and lifted the lid to retrieve the clue. "Okay," I said to Misty as she watched, "I'm ready. Let's see what this clue is," I said as I pulled out the faded parchment.

Unrolling the parchment, my heart sounded like a drum in my ears. Its constant thudding was nearly deafening. I looked at the writing on the page and shrieked.

The door to my room was suddenly full of people. My dad, Scott, had pushed the door open and now his six-four frame was standing in the entrance to my room looking like he was ready to take on any demon that was conspiring to do me harm. His brown eyes scanned every crevice.

My mom, Sandy stood half a step back wringing her hands, her blonde hair was pulled back into a tight braid, and her ice blue eyes conveyed the message that she didn't voice. She was worried about me.

I really couldn't blame them for being so concerned. I had kept the last clue and task a secret until a series of overwhelming anxiety attacks had forced me to let them in.

"What is it?" Mom said softly.

"This," I snapped as I turned the parchment towards them.

Mom and Dad looked at the roll in my hands. "Is that…is that the clue?" Dad inquired softly.

I just shook my head. "Looks like it. It was in the same kind of box the last one was in."

"What language is it in?" my brother Kyle asked as he poked his head in.

"That's what the cry was for," I replied acidly. "Welcome to my life."

Misty decided that she had had enough. She stretched, jumped off of the bed and nudged me as she sat by the door. I got the message, "Okay, girl, let's get you outside." I dropped the parchment on my desk, letting the others look at it while I shuffled to the side of the room and grabbed a sweatshirt.

Five minutes later, I was standing outside watching Misty chase snowflakes. Okay, give her a break-she still thinks she's a puppy. But as I watched, my mind started to work on the clue that I had found this morning.

When this whole endeavor began in September, the first clue had been in Latin. I hadn't recognized it immediately as being Latin, but even then I had known that it was a matter of finding what language it was in and then translating it.

As it turned out, it was a bit more difficult than that. The entire clue had ended up being what my English teacher would call an acrostic. When the clue was written out in English, one sentence per line, the first letters spelled out the actual clue.

The hieroglyphics that were on the scroll currently in my room didn't instill any confidence in my abilities. Well, there was a full three months, until the Spring Equinox, to solve it. And this time, I had more people involved. Not only would I be able to lean on my friends Chris and Emily, my new boyfriend Ian, but also my family.

Regardless of how I looked at this, we were all in this together.

I whistled for Misty. It was time to go in and get ready for the last day of school before the holiday break.

Walking towards the shower, I noticed Kyle's door open slightly and then close just before I walked by. We have an interesting family dynamic.

My brother Kyle and I have always had an challenging relationship. We continue, much to our mother's dismay, to try to out-prank each other. Today, Kyle decided that after the drama from the last week, I needed a laugh.

I had just stepped out of the shower, and was looking at myself in the full-length mirror in the bathroom, and wished that the witch who was responsible for this stupid curse that I was trying to break, had done something nice as a prize for making it through the first step. Really, I wouldn't have argued if she had decided to help me a bit in the looks department.

I mean, my looks are okay. I've got good skin, but my hair constantly looks like the end result of a static electricity demonstration. My waist-length mass of chestnut hair is in a state of constant frizz, regardless of what I try. Coupled with my moss green eyes, I could be pretty, if I'd take the time to work at it. It just seems like it might be more trouble than it's worth, so I don't often get dolled up. Of course, now that Ian and I are dating, I might have to spend a bit more time working on it.

Unfortunately, the rest of me is also lacking a bit in the looks department. I have all the curves of a plank. It just doesn't seem fair, and that was what I was lamenting as I stood in front of the mirror after my shower. I'd beaten the first part of the curse, couldn't she at least give me something?

Shrugging my shoulders, I grabbed my hair dryer from its hook and turned it on.

White smoke billowed all over the room. I looked in the mirror, and I looked like a ghost. Covered in white powder. Again.

It's bad enough that this happens at all. But Kyle had gotten me with this same prank a few months back, and I'd thought I'd been vigilant enough to catch him. But seeing as I was covered, apparently I'd been too distracted today.

"Kyle!" I bellowed. I really didn't have time for this today. "Kyle," I yelled again after I heard his laughter coming through the wall. "Mark my words, you creep, you're going to regret putting baby powder in my hair dryer."

I ripped the plug from the wall, and heaved it into the corner. I ended up getting another glance of myself as I moved.

I had to chuckle. I was quite a sight.

I could only marvel for a moment at my humorous sight. I needed to get into the shower. Again. But I could use the time to plan my revenge. Oh, yes, sweet revenge would be mine.

Running late, due to Kyle's prank, was not putting me in a good mood. I dressed in my favorite jeans and fuzzy sweater and dashed to the kitchen for breakfast.

Mom was flipping what appeared to be slabs of French toast on the griddle, while dad was drinking his habitual cup of coffee while reading the paper. Then there was Kyle; sitting smugly on the stool at the breakfast bar, eating a mound of French toast already drenched in syrup. All the while looking like the cat that got the canary.

I gave him a steely glare.

"Are you heading into the office today, Scott, or are you working from here?" Mom asked while she was fixing a cup of tea.

"I'm going to start off here. I want to finish up the designs for the Emerson Building. I've got a lunch meeting about a new building that we're going to be doing the initial design for. I'll probably swing into the main office to check up on things there," Dad replied.

He's an architect who runs his own company, but found he likes the quiet that he gets from working from home. So a few days a week, he works here only leaving when he has meetings. He does go into his main office in town at least twice a week to check up on how his employees are doing.

"Okay," Mom replied. "I've got to head into the city to meet with Sonja about her editing my new book. I was thinking that perhaps we'd grab lunch together when I got back, but you're already booked. We'll do it another day," she finished as she dropped the plate she had been loading up in front of me at the breakfast bar along with my preferred cup of tea.

My mom works as a freelance writer, so she also works at home. This is usually quite convenient as she is always there when we need her. It also gives her time to indulge herself in what must be her favorite pastime of baking, which means that we have fresh delicious snacks daily. It most certainly works for us.

Just as I was beginning to take that first bite, Dad set down his paper, "Stevie, I'd appreciate it if you would see if your friends could come over this evening after dinner. I'm going to call Nonni and Poppy," he said referring to his parents, "and we'll have everyone over to have the first meeting regarding this new clue."

I gulped, "Sure."

I wondered what else I was going to have to endure today.

Finishing my breakfast, I put my dishes into the dishwasher and got ready to head for the bus station. Pulling on my jacket, I found one of Misty's toys in my pocket, which gave me an idea.

Wagging the squeaky toy just in front of her, I got her worked up into a frenzy. I kept one eye on Kyle, who was currently pulling on his boots while sitting on the deacon's bench. A quick flick of my wrist, and the toy went soaring and landed just behind Kyle. Misty, never taking her eyes off of the prize, followed and landed with four paws scrambling for something to cling to but only finding Kyle's shirt.

"Oops," I said with a slight smile. "Sorry, Kyle."

"Ah, Stevie," he complained. "This was my favorite shirt. Now it's covered in dog hair and slobber."

"She didn't mean it," I said defensively.

Kyle glared at me with eyes as cold as they were icy blue, "She may not have. But you? I have suspicions." He stormed out of the hallway and dashed up to his room for a clean shirt.

Misty sat on the bench, toy held in her mouth, looking at me. I reached over and scratched her ears, "Good girl," I whispered and slipped out the door before Kyle could return.

Walking to the bus stop I took in several deep breaths, marveling in the cold clean air. I knew that I would never take mornings like this for granted ever again.

"Stevie!" a voice cut through my daydream. "Stevie, wait up!"

I turned to see a mass of blue and pink hair sticking out of the hood of a purple parka. "Hey, Emily," I greeted my best friend.

Emily is five-five and a cross between a witch and a fairy. It is impossible to know what style she will be dressed in, as she changes her style to match her daily mood. The only constant that she's had for more than a week has been her hair color, a vibrant blue with pink highlights. She's had that since we were in seventh grade.

I'm really not sure how we ended up becoming best friends. I've known her for what seems to be all of my life, but we are so totally opposite of each other. She's got those really well defined curves that everyone wants, she's agile enough to be athletic if she wants and she's able to keep fantastic control of her emotions. I on the other hand have a temper problem that recently got me a few nights of detention and due to the damage I cause from being so accident-prone three demolition companies are actively trying to recruit me.

The other area where we are polar opposites is in our demeanor. I've always been kind of quiet and shy, preferring to be a loner. Emily had no problem letting people know she's in the room.

She threw her arms around me and gave me a hug so tight that I could barely breathe. "Thanks for figuring it out," she said almost crying. "I was so afraid that I'd get a call this morning, that you know..." She didn't finish the sentence, but we both knew what she meant.

Releasing me, she leaned back, "So what did you have to do?"

I chuckled a little. It was easy to laugh about it now, but last night when I had been so worried it hadn't been any kind of laughing matter. "I had to be honest with myself," I stated matter-of-factually.

"But you were always honest with yourself, weren't you?"

"On most things," I said as I pulled the edge of my hat down further over my ears. "But when it came to things with Ian, I kept trying to delude myself."

"Ian, huh?" Emily's deep blue eyes bored into mine. "Do tell."

Caught, and feeling slightly embarrassed, I tried to put it into words. "I've had feelings for him for a while, but I wouldn't admit it or try to follow through on them," I said exasperated. "I told you that he had asked me out the other day, right?"

"Yeah, and then you said that you told him that you needed to focus on the task. That sounds pretty honest to me," Emily said.

"It was. Almost," I whispered as I hung my head slightly. "I really wanted to go out with him, but kept thinking of the bigger goal. Then, last night it hit me that what I really wanted was to say yes to him. To take that chance and see where it would go. I nearly didn't make it."

"Made your decision too late?"

"In a way. I called his house right after I figured it out, but he wasn't home. His mom didn't know where he was or when he'd be home. His cell phone was off and going right to voice mail. Needless to say, I panicked. I found myself in the car, driving aimlessly and ended up at the edge of the woods of the Hollow. I followed my intuition and found him at the boulder where I ended up yesterday after my panic attack." I looked up with a smile on my face, "We got everything resolved with about an hour to spare," I said triumphantly.

The bus turned onto the street, and the rest of the students started to surge forward. "I'm happy for you," Emily said as she pulled me in for another hug.

I noticed another figure running down the street, and my smile grew. "Looks like Kyle might make the bus after all," I muttered.

As we straightened and made our way to the queue, Emily asked, "Is his being late your fault?"

"Me? No. Misty jumped on him and messed up his shirt just before we were ready to leave."

Apparently Emily saw the sparkle in my eye. "Stevie, what did you do to get that pup to jump on your brother?"

I just laughed as we got on the bus. I told her my version of Kyle's morning adventure and we shared in the laugh. Today was going to be okay.

CHAPTER 2

READY

Chugging up the final hill, the bus rounded the bend in the road and Sleepy Hollow High came into view. Like many things in my life that I had just accepted as things that would always be there, I looked at the school through new eyes.

Faded brick walls topped with a white concrete molding, formed the horseshoe-shaped building. A solitary flagpole sat in the middle of the little island that was created by the bus loop, and a sign that proclaimed this as the home of the Horsemen sat just in front of the pole facing the road.

It was a little surreal, pulling in today. I had been here last night, but hadn't been certain that I would see it again this morning.

As the bus slowed, I started looking out the windows for familiar faces. It hit me then and I turned to Emily, "Chris wasn't at the bus stop this morning. Did you hear from him?"

Emily's eyes widened. "You're right. I was so caught up with what's been going on with you, that I totally forgot." She too looked around, searching for his familiar face. "Maybe his mom gave him a ride today?" she asked hopefully.

Chris was the third member of our long-standing trio. He'd joined us when we were in first grade, and we've pretty much been the three-amigos since. Chris is quiet and shy like me, and about my height with fine features. He keeps his red hair longish, but not as long as my boyfriend Ian's who wears his in a ponytail. Chris had always been a very stylish dresser until about a year ago. For some reason around last Christmas, he suddenly started wearing clothing that was really baggy.

Chris' life hadn't been easy, and right now it seemed there were nightly issues between him and his stepfather, Mark. All I could do was hope that everything was all right and that he was just running late today.

Throngs of students were pushing their ways from the unloading buses towards the two main doors of the school. I kept searching the faces amid the crowd, looking for two in particular. My eyes fixed on one, Ian, just before a snowball exploded over my head and showered me in a fine coating of the white powder.

"Hey, Stevie. Emily," Ian greeted us. He pulled me in and gave me a quick kiss. I felt the temperature of my body soar because my blood was boiling.

"Hi, Ian," I nearly purred. "Glad to see you this morning."

"Me too," he said quietly as he turned me, but kept his arm firmly around my waist. We began walking up the steps to the entrance. We were almost inside, when he seemingly asked out of the blue, "Where's Chris today?"

"We were thinking the same thing when we got off of the bus. He wasn't at the stop this morning. Maybe his mom brought him in, or he had an appointment that he didn't mention to us," Emily summed up as we made our way to our lockers.

Ian walked me to my locker before he proceeded the rest of the way to his own. I quickly stashed my coat, opting to wear my Uggs for the day instead of changing into sneaks, and pulled out what I needed for orchestra today. As I stood up and looked towards Ian's locker, he was walking back towards me, and the ball in my stomach tightened again.

Ice shards still shone in Ian's auburn hair. He wore it longer, much longer, than was fashionable. Today he'd pulled it back into a simple ponytail that fell to his mid back. His skin was pale, but not a sickly color and today he wore a shirt that matched the color of his eyes, sky blue.

I'd met Ian shortly after he had moved into the district. He had inadvertently found out about the first clue and task that we had been working on, and had integrated himself into the fabric of our lives without anyone getting seriously alarmed. In retrospect, it was almost like he'd used the puppy-dog-sales-closing method: you take the pup home for a "test-drive" and you end up getting attached. Ian had never forced himself into the group; he just started being there, answering questions, allaying fears and helping with the task. The next thing we knew, he was one of us.

Over the past three months, Ian had been my rock. He was the one that had always remained calm, regardless of what was happening. He has such compassion that it literally overwhelms me sometimes. It's like his innate setting seems to be set for caring about others. This was one of the main reasons that I had found myself falling in love with Ian. He was one of those rare people, especially teen-aged, who genuinely cared for others around him.

And for whatever reason, and frankly right now I didn't care what the reason was, he had found me attractive. His tenacity to woo me had only been outshone by his concern for me during the last task. He'd let me set the pace, and I'd nearly blown it. Now, I was determined that I was going to make every moment with him count.

He walked slowly back to where I stood just outside of my locker, with his eyes fixed on only one thing: me. How had I ever deluded myself into thinking that ignoring our feelings for each other was going to be the right choice?

"He looks like he'd like to take a big bite out of only you," Emily's voice came from over my shoulder. I'd been so entranced by Ian, I hadn't even noticed that she'd come up behind me.

"Yeah, he does," I agreed. "And to be honest, I'd like to take one out of him too."

"Amen to that," Emily said as Ian joined us.

Without a word, he came around so he could stand on my left, and took my oboe and folder. His right hand snaked out and took my left hand, and we began walking towards the orchestra room.

"I texted Chris before I came back here to meet you two," Ian said as we neared the main hallway. "I still haven't heard back from him. I hope everything is all right."

"Thanks, for checking on him," I said as we walked around a gaggle of freshman who were standing in the halls laughing about something. "Oh, there is something that I need to talk to all of you about," I said as I nudged Emily. "My dad wants to have a big pow-wow tonight to start looking at the next clue."

"The next clue? Oh shoot, how could we have forgotten about that?" Emily asked. "I mean, I was just so happy to see you here, I totally forgot that we're not out of the woods yet."

"Yeah, and while I do prefer looking at trees from this side, I'm still on the clock. Anyway, my dad wants to get everyone together and start on this as soon as possible. So, if we could get together at my place, say around seven-thirty?"

Emily nodded her answer as she ducked into her first period class. Ian, pulled me close just outside the orchestra door, and gave me a kiss that made my toes tingle. "I'll see you in Physics. And I'll let my mom know about tonight," he said as he walked away and left me standing in the hall staring after him.

Gathered around the lunch table, Ian, Emily and I poured over the roll of parchment that I had found this morning. Ian looked at the hieroglyphics with a tentative look. Obviously, he had never encountered anything like this before, but he kept running his fingertips over one design in particular.

"Any thoughts?" I finally asked.

"These don't look like the ones that we saw when we were studying the ancient Egyptians. I don't think that they are from that time period," Emily verbalized her thoughts.

I just shook my head. I agreed with her, but felt totally out of my element here.

Ian again leaned down and popped his glasses up so he could get a better view of one symbol. "I think," he started. "I think that I've seen this one somewhere before." He looked at it carefully, still perplexed.

I could see it when an idea popped into his head. "Stevie, would you have a problem if I took a picture of this one symbol? I think I saw it on something that came from my grandmother's house. My mom might have an idea of what it is," he said looking over at me.

"S-s-sure, I guess," I stammered. I couldn't see how a picture of a single symbol would help, but, hey, I'm open to any ideas. I was also surprised that, once again, Ian thought that a family member would be able to help with the solution of the clue.

Ian pulled out his cell phone and took a picture of the entire parchment, and then a close up of the symbol that he was particularly interested in.

Jumping at the bell, we quickly rolled the parchment back up. Emily grabbed the trash from the table and ran it over to one of the dumpsters that sat along the wall. Ian and I finished putting everything else into my book bag.

Holding Ian's hand we made our way over to where Emily was waiting near the exit. It was then that I saw Ian's cousin Gabby Sosong standing with her friend Tanya Spitz at one of the tables. Gabby looked like she had just swallowed something that had gone incredibly sour in her mouth; her eyes bulged and her lips puckered. I could see that she was staring at Ian and I.

"Don't look now," I whispered to Ian, "but I think your cousin is going to want to have a serious talk with you after she rips my head off."

Ian glanced over, smiled and gave Gabby a quick wave.

I thought she was going to explode with the rage that was on her face. She and I had never been close. I had a bad feeling my being with her cousin wasn't going to improve our relationship.

An hour later, I entered Mrs. Vallente's History class. The first person I saw was Gabby standing with Tanya near the desk that I shared with Emily.

"Oh wonderful," I muttered under my breath so that only Emily would hear.

"What?" she began to say before she saw the two of them. "What do you think they want?" she nearly whined. Emily was at about the same level with Gabby and Tanya as I was. Seeing them waiting for us was stressful.

As I got close to the table, Gabby looked at me, "Hey, Nixon," she said in her trademarked soft tone that was underwritten with violence. "I saw you holding hands with my nerdy cousin. You two going steady now?"

I gulped. "We're dating, yes," I managed to say keeping my voice steadier than I felt.

"You screw him up, I'll screw you up," Gabby said. She looked intently into my eyes.

I just nodded.

Her grimace gave way to a slight grin, "I guess I need to say thanks for what you and the nerd did for me and Tanya. My aunt let my mom know. So thanks." She and Tanya walked over to their table and took their seats without so much as another look at Emily and I.

"Okay," I muttered as I pulled out my chair and took my seat. "That was just plain weird."

"Yeah," Emily whispered in agreement. "I wonder what got into them?"

Like most of my other classes today, Mrs. Vallente was letting us use this one as a make up day for people to catch up with any work before we went on vacation. Since Emily and I were totally caught up, this essentially gave us a free period.

We took time to quietly discuss the clue, trying out different theories, but since other people were using the computers to finish up class work, we couldn't do much. "Do you think Ian will have much luck with this?" Emily asked referring to the symbol that he had been so focused on during lunch.

"I don't know. It'd be nice to get a good start on the clue this time. I really hate the thought of needing to spend so much time working on the clue. Everything got too close for comfort this last time."

Emily nodded, "Yeah, I can understand that." She thought for a moment, "Hey, did Ian say if he ever heard back from Chris?"

"No. And that's got me worried. Even when he's sick for a day, he finds a way to send a quick message to let us know what's going on." I thought for a moment, "I hope he and Mark didn't have another go around," I said referring to Chris' stepfather.

Emily thought for a moment, "Yeah, Mark is okay, but he and Chris seem to have different opinions about what it means to be a guy, you know."

"You're right about that," I responded. I thought about my friend who wasn't any taller than I was, and had roughly the same build. I knew that his stepfather was an ex-Army Ranger, now a self-employed construction worker, who kept trying to build Chris into his version of what a man should be. "I just hope everything is okay."

I was glad at the end of the class that, for whatever reason, Gabby and Tanya had given Emily and I a reprieve from the normal teasing and mild abuse that they normal showered us

with. It was a little disconcerting, but I was thankful for it.
Perhaps doing the right thing had laid a very shaky foundation
between my personal nemesis and myself. Or maybe it was just
because of the holiday season. Whatever the reason, I'd take it.

When the bell rang, I headed out, and saw Gabby had beaten
me out of the room, and was now talking with her cousin. I kept
back a ways. It was obvious that she was giving him the third
degree, but he kept his back straight and never cowed in front of
her.

He said something to her that suddenly had her mouth
opening and closing like a landed trout. I almost wanted to laugh
at her face but thought better of if.

Ian walked towards me, still chuckling under his breath and
shaking his head. Reaching out, he took my hand and spun me in
closer. The kiss he gave me made me forget the little interaction
that I had just witnessed between him and Gabby. "Did you
have a good class, Stevie?" he crooned.

"Yeah. It wasn't too bad. I spent most of the time talking to
Em. Your cousin even left me alone for the most part," I said. I
remembered how she had looked just before she walked away.
"By the way what did you say to her that had her looking like a
hooked fish?"

Ian's laugh was smoky and low, and immediately I wished
that I could hear it more often. "I just reminded her of some

personal information that my aunt would be very shocked to hear, and that if she kept giving me, or you for that matter, any trouble I'd see to it that that information got delivered." There was a twinkle in his eye that made me think of a saying that my dad said when I was young; *when Irish eyes are smiling, they're usually up to something.*

We were now standing in front of Mr. Sweeny's room. Ian leaned over, and gave me another quick kiss. "I'll meet you at your locker. Then we can go over to Scoops and grab a hot cocoa before I drive you home, okay?" He again had that twinkle in his eye.

"Sounds good to me," I said as I backed into my math class.

All I had to do was survive the next fifty minutes, and then I could begin to relax on my vacation.

Taking comfort in that fact, I found my seat and plopped into it without any grace at all. My mind was already taking the afternoon off. Mr. Sweeny had us watching a video of sports commentators talking about how using math and science would help us improve our playing abilities.

I really didn't pay much attention to the video. First, I knew all of the relationships that they were talking about from physics, but more importantly I knew me. I was the klutz who not that long ago injured four people with a single swing of my tennis racquet. If I got any better, I could work with Chris' stepfather as a one-woman wrecking crew.

I let my mind wander. I kept watching the clock, waiting impatiently for the day to be over so I could go out with Ian and enjoy some alone time. I knew that I still had a major obligation that I had to see through. But, unlike the first clue, this time I had my own army ready to help with whatever I needed. I was scared, sure, but I felt ready to take on the upcoming task.

CHAPTER 3

UNSURPRISING NEW YEAR

Vacation was a blur of days that seemed to follow a fairly prescribed routine: get up when I was ready, have breakfast, go out to the shop and work on my Sonex homebuilt airplane for the rest of the morning. Since my friends were more tuned into the afternoon hours than mornings, I was able to get quite a bit done prior to meeting up with them after lunch.

My schedule after lunch was pretty much set as well. Ian, Emily and Chris would usually arrive at my house around noon. My mom would make a pot of soup and the group of us, along with my brother, would sit around the table and play cards while we ate. After lunch, Kyle would head out to meet up with his friends, leaving the rest of us to work on solving the clue.

Unfortunately, we hadn't been able to make much progress on this clue. Ian and I had searched through several books on ancient hieroglyphics, and had found nothing useable. Emily had been researching various cultures that had used pictures as forms of writing. She had had nearly as much luck as Ian and I had.

The weird part of things had been Chris. With the last clue, he had been an integral part of the team. This round, he seemed to be very distracted. Something told me that there were extenuating circumstances that were pulling at him. In truth, I was very worried about him.

During one of the library excursions that Ian and I had taken into Mercy College, we had seen Chris, meeting with some people on the campus. We didn't get a chance to talk to him, but Ian and I spent the ride home philosophizing about what he was doing there. When we saw him the next day and mentioned seeing him, he denied that he had been there.

All in all, the time spent being off of school had pretty much led us no closer to unraveling the clue from the witch, and had only left us with more questions.

"Ian," I complained as we left the library for the fifth time this week, "I feel as though I'm spinning my wheels on this clue."

"Relax a bit, Stevie," he said as her squeezed my hand. "It took us a while to figure out the first clue. It makes sense that it is going to take quite a bit of energy to get the second resolved."

I thought about what he said. "Yeah," I said, "I guess you're right. It wouldn't make sense for this clue to be easier than the first."

Walking through the great oak door into the cold air I felt like I was escaping the evil dungeon where a vindictive witch was holding me captive. Okay, that's figuratively speaking, but still the reality was not that far off. I was already through nearly two weeks of the thirteen that I would have to solve this clue and complete the associated task. I was all too aware of the time that had elapsed. I was even more aware of the penalty for failure. I'm not afraid of death; I'm just not ready to experience it. Just thinking about it left me slightly nauseous.

Ian's phone let out a shrill sound, which broke my train of thought. I wandered over to the railing and stared out towards the Hudson River and let the myriad of thoughts that were bouncing around in my skull continue to ricochet, hoping that they would suddenly fall into some semblance of order. As if I could be that lucky.

I must have been totally absorbed in my own thoughts while Ian was on the phone, since I didn't hear him come up from behind me.

"You okay?" he asked as he touched my coat sleeve.

I jumped at the touch and spun around holding my hand over my wide-open mouth.

Gently, Ian pulled me into his arms. "It's okay, Stevie. I didn't mean to startle you," he cooed in a very soothing voice.

The sob that had frozen in my throat finally made it out, and I embarrassed myself by clutching him and burying my face into his jacket. I don't know how long it took for me to settle down, but he never showed any signs of impatience.

When I felt that I could finally talk, I lifted my head enough so that the jacket didn't hinder my mouth, "I'm sorry about that, Ian."

He gently rubbed my back in soothing circles. "To tell the truth, I've been expecting something along these lines. You've been handling everything so stoically; I just figured that it was a matter of time before it all caught up with you."

Holding me close, he said, "I'll listen if you'd like to spew about it all. I can't say that I'd have any answers, but it might help to get everything off of your chest."

I looked into his ice blue eyes, and like always, was lost. He wouldn't bully me into revealing all of my fears and concerns, but I could see that he wanted to take some of the burden off of me. Right then I gave up all pretensions of trying to brave it out on my own.

"Aside from the obvious problem of working out the clue, I'm really getting worried about Chris," I said. "I don't know how much you know about him, but he's had a pretty rough life so far." I turned and took Ian's hand and started walking down one of the many sidewalks that led from the library.

"Chris's dad was killed in Iraq when he was just five. He and his mom, Joyce, moved back here so they could be closer to her family." I paused and gazed into the clear night sky and tried to pull strength from the moon that was just over the treetops.

"I can definitely relate to that," Ian said quietly.

"I'm sorry. I didn't mean to make you think about your dad's passing." I squeezed his hand hoping it would comfort him.

"It's okay," he said with a thin smile. "What happened next?"

"Joyce has done everything that she could to make his life easier. A few years ago, she met and married Mark Brown. Mark's an okay guy, an ex-ranger who now runs his own construction company. Unfortunately, he and Chris don't exactly see eye-to-eye on several issues."

"Like what?"

"Well," I continued, "you may have noticed that Chris is not a very aggressive guy; he's rather docile. He hangs out with mostly girls, but he's not interested in dating any of us. Mark is his polar opposite. He is extremely competitive and often shows a bit of aggression.”

“They had a huge blow up late last year. Up until last Christmas, Chris had always dressed conservatively, almost in a preppy style. Then suddenly, he began wearing baggy jeans and shirts. Mark was not happy at all about this. It was almost a month before they were able to work everything out and even then, it took Joyce hauling the two of them to a shrink. Since then, things have been a little better, but Mark still jumps on him at the slightest things.”

I sighed. “Chris and I have known each other since third grade. We became fast friends; him, Emily and I. We’ve been almost inseparable since then. But something has changed recently, and I don’t know what’s wrong or how I can help. Since just before the holidays, Chris has become withdrawn and hasn’t been spending as much time with us. I talked to Em the other day, and neither of us understands. We’ve both tried talking to him, but we’ve made no progress.”

We were back at the car by the time I had finished telling Ian about Chris’s background. Instead of opening the door, he pulled me into his strong arms and we leaned against the car. “I haven’t known Chris all that long, but I’ve seen some of what you were referring to in the past few months. About all we can do is be his friends and be ready to help him when he needs it," Ian said. I just nodded, and snuggled in closer.

Lying in bed that night, I scratched Misty behind the ear. "I wish I knew what was going on with Chris. Guess time will tell," I said in a sleepy voice just before I closed my eyes.

The dreams that came that night were definitely not of the settling type. I felt I was running through the woods chasing someone. I kept calling, but I couldn't see who it was that I was after. I was only able to catch glimmers of a woman with her long fire-red hair billowing out behind her.

Just as I got close enough so that I could hear her breathing, I called out one last time. She turned and looked at me with a face that was as familiar as it was strange. And then she jumped off of the cliff.

"Stevie!" my mom's voice cut through the fog of my mind and I felt her shaking my arm. "Stevie, wake up honey. You're having a nightmare."

I opened my eyes and sucked in a breath. "What happened?"

My mom flipped on the bedside light, and sat on the edge of the bed and pulled me into her arms. "Shouldn't I be asking you? You were thrashing and yelling so that you woke your dad and me."

I looked around the room. Misty was curled in the corner of the bed, whimpering while my dad stood in the doorway. He had the phone in his hand, ready to dial for help if I needed it. Inhaling slowly I tried to calm myself down. "I guess I had a whale of a nightmare," I stated and then proceeded to tell them as much as I could remember.

"Do you think it has anything to do with the clue this time?" my dad asked.

I just shrugged. "I dunno. Maybe, but it all seems so unrelated."

Mom thought for a minute, "Did you recognize the woman you were following?"

"She looked familiar, like I've seen her before, but I don't know her. At least I don't think I do."

Ducking through the hallway after first period the next morning to avoid the scrutiny of Gabby and her motley crew, I saw a familiar red stub of a ponytail. I reached out and gave it a quick tug. "Hey, Chris. Wait up a sec."

Chris' shoulders slumped a bit, but he stopped and turned towards me. "Hey, Stevie."

I could hardly believe my eyes. His normally bright hazel eyes were flat, and his cheeks looked sallow. The dark bags under his eyes looked big enough to pack everything for a family of six for a two-week vacation. "Chis," I gasped, "What's going on?"

Tears formed in the corners of his eyes. Quickly swiping at them with the cuff of his sweater, he shook his head. "I can't talk about it. At least not here, Stevie. I'm okay, really."

"Christopher Lehr, I believe that may be the first lie you've told me since we met in elementary school. I've known you too long to believe it," I scolded. "If you can't talk about it now, let's meet after school, just you and me, and let me know what's going on." I reached out, and pulled him in for a hug, "You're my best friend, Chris, let me help however I can. Please?"

Everything looked blurry to me, and I realized that my own eyes were wet. But finally I saw what I needed to see. Chris nodded.

"I'll meet you after school, but not at Scoops. Let's go to the coffee shop on Cedar, okay?"

"I'll be there, Chris." I squeezed him tight and then let him go and watched him walk down the hall looking forlorn.

Sitting in the cafeteria that afternoon, I mindlessly picked at my sandwich while Ian and Emily watched silently. "You going to spew and let us know what's eating you or are you planning to just mope all day?" Emily asked.

I looked over at her, sighed and shoved my mutilated sandwich away. "I talked to Chris this morning. He looks like hell," I announced gloomily.

"Yeah," Ian agreed. "I saw him in history, and he didn't look good. I wanted to talk to him after class, but he disappeared right at the bell."

Emily's eyes traced from me to Ian and back. "We've got to do something. Maybe we need to have an intervention or something."

Looking up fro the table for the first time, "I'm meeting with him tonight after school."

"Okay, then I'll call you after dinner, and you can fill me in."

"Em, I'm going to try to get him to tell me what's going on. I'm going to promise to keep his secrets if he needs me to." Knowing that she was going to protest, I held up my hands, "I promise that I will try to convince him that we can all help, but I need to keep his confidence."

Ian draped his arm over my shoulders and pulled my in closer. Kissing the top of my head, "You're a special girl, Stevie. I know that you'll do whatever you can to help Chris tonight. But I'm asking you to let us know how we can help as well. I don't want to see you run headlong into the wall because you are trying to solve Chris' problem single-handedly as well as taking care of the clue."

At three-thirty that afternoon, I was sitting at a small table in the corner of Le Coffee. I'd never been here before but the place seemed comfortable enough. I sipped at my chai tea latte, and watched the door for Chris.

He was later than I had expected, and when he came in, he continued looking over his shoulder as if trouble was following him. Now I became even more concerned.

He stomped his feet to knock off the snow, and looked around the room quickly. Before I could signal to him, he started weaving his way through the small crowd of our classmates who were in line at the counter.

"Hi, Chris."

"Hey, Stevie. Thanks for meeting me down here." He dropped into the chair like he'd been stunned, and laid his head on the table.

I could see his shoulders jerking, a sure sign that he was crying, but trying not to let anyone else know. I squeezed his hand tightly, and was relieved to feel him grip my hand too. "Chris," I whispered nearly in tears myself, "what's going on?"

He held my hand tight for a few moments while he fought to regain his composure. He sat up a little, wiped his eyes and took a steadying breath. "Things haven't been good between Mark and me for a while," he began. "That's not exactly news, but it's where this story begins."

"Mark got on me about a year ago when I started dressing this way. Since then, he's been very critical about everything that I do. Well, right after Christmas, he barged into my room while I was on the computer. I was...," he paused trying to figure out where to go.

"Where you checking out girls on one of those porn sites?" I asked offhandedly trying to lighten the mood.

"Not exactly."

Well that surprised me. "What do you mean not exactly, Chris?"

"He found me ordering some pills off of the Internet, Stevie."

"Pills!" I nearly shrieked. "Chris, why in heavens are you ordering pills off of the Internet? Don't you have any idea how dangerous that is?" I saw how his face dropped, and forced myself to take a few cleansing breaths. "I'm sorry, Chris. I can see that this is very hard for you, and me flying off of the handle there didn't make it any better." I took a steadying breath and then asked, "What pills were you ordering?"

"Ones that I need, and ones that Mark is fighting me about." He watched my face, waiting for a reaction. "Listen, Stevie, I know it sounds bad, but the company is a reputable one that delivers good merchandise."

"Are you addicted to these drugs?" I asked.   An addiction would explain the recent mood swings, and the bizarre behavior.

"They're not addictive drugs, Stevie.   They're just hormones, but I need them.   When Mark found out, he absolutely flipped out on me."

"What happened?"

"Before or after he called my mom?" he gave a slight laugh. "Let's see, he threatened to beat the living daylights out of me, then he and my mom dragged me off to the doctor's office which led us to a psychiatrist at the university."

"So that's why I saw you there.   Why didn't you say anything?"

"This is a big problem in our house right now.   Mark's trying to convince my mom to have me admitted to a mental hospital."

"What did your mom say?"

"Oh, let's just say that she is supremely ticked that I went behind her back and have been ordering those pills for the last two years.   And of course, she wasn't thrilled with the results; from either the doctors or the pills."

I thought for a minute, sipped my tea and let what Chris had just said sink in.   "Chris, you said that the story begins with when you started wearing the baggy clothes.   I guess I'm not following you too well, but I'm not seeing how everything is related."

"I started wearing the clothes to help cover the results from the pills." He was shaking slightly.

I reached over and put a hand on his arm. "You okay? Do you need a hit or something?"

He smiled, a real smile that reached his eyes. "I'm scared right now, Stevie. Everything is coming to a head right now, and I don't have any idea how long it'll be before it all blows over. I can't tell you much more than I have right now. My mom and Mark have threatened to send me away if I tell anyone what's going on until we know all of the specifics."

I smiled back at him, squeezed his arm again, "Remember that we are here for you. Come back and let us help however we can."

"I'll try, I promise," he looked at his watch. "I've got another appointment with the shrink today, and my mom is meeting me here in a few."

I nodded, knowing that right now he didn't want her to find that we had been talking. "Take care of yourself, Chris. Let me know if I can help in any way."

We hugged and then I headed for the door. I needed time to think before I did anything else, so I headed for the woods behind the school. Chris needed friends to support him through whatever was going on. But pushing for answers would only drive him away from us.

I pulled out my phone, called Ian and planned to meet him and Emily in a half hour in the school parking lot.

Trudging through the snow, I knew I had a lot to deal with. I waited until I got to the large rock in the woods and boosted myself up onto a clear area and pulled my knees up. I was still trying to work out the next clue for my personal quest, but the clues that Chris had given me seemed much more important right now.

Pulling up Google, I typed in "hormones" and got a bunch of stuff about hormones that our bodies need to keep us going. Nothing earth-shattering there. And a lot of them can cause mood swings and possible weight gain. Chris had said that he wore the baggy clothes to hide the effects of the pills. What kind of hormones would alter a body's physical appearance?

A few more queries and I had a horrible feeling I had found my answer – *sex hormones*. But why would Chris need them?

CHAPTER 4

UNTHINKABLE

Time seemed to fly by over the next week. Any time that I wasn't in school, I was either working with Ian, Emily and occasionally Chris on trying to decipher the clue. I had given Ian and Emily only superfluous information from my meeting with Chris. They only knew that there were severe problems for him at home, and that he, his mom and Mark were working with professionals to resolve them.

I had done a little more research on why a boy might need male hormones and what would happen if a male took female hormones. And honestly, if my suspicion was correct, it was more than weight gain that Chris was hiding.

"Did you see this?" Emily asked as she dropped a paper on the counter.

"I only look at the comics and the crossword puzzle in the paper. The rest of it is too depressing."

She pointed to the lead article on the front page.

MOB KILLS GAY STUDENT

Suddenly my throat seemed very constricted. I snatched the paper away and scanned the article. "My God," I murmured. My eyes focused on Emily's face, "I can't believe that they killed this poor kid just because of his sexual orientation."

"You and I may not see it as a big deal, but I have a cousin who is gay and his father won't even talk to him. Homophobia is a problem, Stevie."

Pulling on all of my inner strength, I fought to keep my outward appearance calm. I could feel the butterflies in my stomach tying themselves into knots. If Chris was taking sex hormones, specifically female hormones, what did that make him? Gay? A transvestite?

I stared out the window into the falling snow. There had to be someway to find out more of what was going on with Chris while not giving away his secret. But I was scared; I didn't want anything to happen to him.

The sound of my door opening snapped me from my thoughts, and I turned towards the kitchen door. "Ian! Chris!"

Pulling off his snow covered wool cap, Ian shook his head like a wet dog and sent a spray of cold wet snow streaming off of his ponytail.

"Ewww," Emily squealed as she leapt back in an attempt to avoid be hit with the spray.

Grabbing a handful of ice from the floor, I walked over to Ian, and while his arms were struggling to get free of his coat, I stuffed it down his back.

"Oh that's cold, Stevie," he said as he shrugged out of the coat and tried to fish the melting snow out of his shirt.

I winked over at Chris, and was surprised to see that he had a smile on his face. And for the first time in a week it didn't look like it had been forced there. Hanging their coats on the pegs by the door I asked them, "So, what brings you guys around today?"

Without missing a beat, Chris looked at me and replied, "Ian's car."

"I should have expected an answer like that," I murmured as I stepped back into the kitchen. "So, if we can try to dispense with the comical comments, maybe one of you'd like to answer the question."

Ian smiled and turned back into the hall and grabbed a bag from the nearest pastry shop. "Figured that you'd be working on the clue and all today, so I thought I'd grab Chris, a dozen doughnuts and we'd make it a party and see if we can't make some headway today." He paused for a second, "Although, with the cold reception I was welcomed with maybe I won't give you one," he said with a wicked grin on his face.

With a grin on my own face that probably matched his, I marched over, grabbed the shoulders of his shirt and planted a kiss on his lips. "I hope that that payment will cover the cost of my silly behavior earlier," I cooed.

His eyes were still glazed over when I let go of him and he staggered two steps before he caught his balance. "I'd say that payment was made in full, and I may even owe you some change," he said while pulling me in for another round.

"Listen," Emily said, "I'm glad you two are working on your financial bookkeeping and all, but I've got to be out of here in just about three hours. If we are going to work on the clue, great, otherwise, I may just decide to head off a little early."

Three hours later, I was brushing my hair out of my eyes, yet again; I looked at the pile of papers that we had compiled. We had all worked steadily at the task at hand, but it still seemed to me that we were fighting a battle without having the weapons. I could feel the frustration boiling up inside of me, and I knew that I was going to need to walk away from this very soon. Preferably before I said something that I was going to regret later.

"Relax, Stevie," Ian said. "We're getting there. We've been over a dozen ideas on what this could be."

"Yeah," I snapped, "a dozen ideas and we still don't have it. All we have is a dozen ways that this doesn't work. We're no closer to solving this than we were three hours ago!" I could feel the tears forming in my eyes.

Ian pushed the piles of paper towards the center of the table, as he scooted his chair closer to me. Wrapping his arms around me, he pulled me in closer and rested my head on his chest.

I could feel his lips softly kissing the top of my head. "Stevie," he said, "you're right, but wrong at the same time. Today we found a dozen ways that didn't work. But remember, no is still an answer. Today we eliminated a dozen possibilities. Our list is down by twelve. Therefore, we are closer."

He held me there, neither of us speaking. My breathing steadied and I could feel my lungs release so that I could take a full breath again.

I broke the silence, "Ian, I'm a little worried about Chris, and more specifically his safety."

Ian shifted slightly, "What's going on that I don't know about, Stevie?"

"I'm not really sure. But did you see this morning's paper? About the kid over in New Paltz who was beaten?"

"I saw it, but I really didn't pay too much attention to it. What happened?"

"From what I read, the kid came out as gay at his school. The people who he thought were his friends; the ones he was counting on to support him, they turned on him. They formed a mob, and beat him. To death."

I knew that Ian was thinking by the way his fingers kept tracing ovals on my arms. "Do you think that Chris is gay?" he finally asked.

"I'm not sure what I think." I stopped and forced myself to edit out certain pieces of information that Chris had told me in confidence. "There is just too much to this, and maybe because it is all happening at the same time, I'm just projecting. It's probably nothing."

"Have you considered talking to Principal Lerch?" Ian asked.

"What am I going to do, walk into her office and say 'Hey Principal Lerch, can we set up a GBLT group here because I've got a friend who's ordering meds online and I think he needs support'?"

Ian spun me around, "What was that about ordering meds online?"

Oh blast it all! I wasn't suppose to say anything about that, and in my frustration, it had slipped out. "I was just spouting off, that's all, Ian." I hoped that he'd buy it.

He looked me right in the eye, "Stevie, you know that I love you. And I know that you know that I know that you've been hiding something about what's going on with Chris. Now, would I be correct that he is ordering pills from the Internet?"

I hung my head; I was caught and I knew it. There was nothing that I could do and be truthful to both of my friends. I nodded as the tears began streaming down my cheeks and I pushed my face into Ian's chest and cried.

When I was done, Ian asked me to tell him the whole story. With his promise to keep it between just us, I did. When I was done, I did feel a bit better. Maybe talking to Ms. Lerch would be the best answer.

Catching up with Ms. Lerch proved to be problematic over the next two days. I was informed by Mrs. Croft that she was attending a seminar out of town and wouldn't be back until after the weekend. Thinking that the Vice-Principal could help, I went to see Mr. Bigelow after school.

"Stevie, I admire your ideas," he said, "but unfortunately I can't do anything at this time."

"Why not?" I stammered.

"Well, for several reasons." Leaning back in his chair, his folded hands on his lap, he looked me square in the eye. "First, the School board is tightening our budget, especially in the areas of clubs and activities. Second, in order for us to have a club of any kind, we must have a faculty member who is willing to be in charge of it. And lastly, Mrs. Lerch is in control of the creation of all clubs and interest groups here at Sleepy Hollow High."

"So," I asked with a tremor in my voice, "what I need to do is find a faculty member who is willing to chair this group, find a way that we can be self-sufficient, or have enough reasons to convince others that we need to spend money on this, and then bring everything back to Mrs. Lerch. Is that correct?"

"Simply put, yes. I'm sorry Stevie, and I do wish you well on this project. After what happened not far from here, I think we need to do something." He paused, and I could see he was contemplating something. He took out a post-it and wrote down a few notes on the paper and slid it across to me. "These are a few teachers that I know who might be willing to help with this, as well as a website that I've heard about that might be of use as well. Good luck." He stood, so I knew that the meeting was over.

Leaving the building, I cut through the parking lot and was surprised to see a large number of cars circled around a group of kids at the far end of the lot. I walked towards the group cautiously. I started to pick out various students in the group from the way that they were dressed, or by the color of their hair. Let's face it; a blue Mohawk is pretty distinguishable.

As I crept nearer, their voices started to span the distance, so I stopped and listened without intruding. I knew that this seemed rude, but it was just plain weird that there would be a group of students hanging out at this time of day on a winter's afternoon. It almost seemed to be some type of pep rally. I listened more intently, trying to pick out words as opposed to just the tenor of the sound.

"If they're different than us, they gotta go!" one voice yelled.

"Are we going to take them starting to form groups in our school?" another shouted.

That question was answered with a resounding, "Hell no!" Hearing this triggered a switch in my mind that said they were bordering on a mob mentality. That meant it was time for me to start moving out. But as I backed away I heard the volume of the shouts rise.

"Where we gonna start?" a female's voice asked.

"Hey, that Reynolds queer works down at the Café. Let's start there."

I felt a cold pit of fear where my stomach used to be. Damian Reynolds was a funny guy who was a year younger than me. He had an infectious toothy grin, skin the color of hot cocoa, and he was openly gay.

"Yeah that works," someone yelled. "Take care of the problem, and then we can grab a bite to eat!"

I quickly maneuvered my way around to the shelter side of the building. I needed time to think. A glance at the teacher's lot dashed my hopes that there would be someone there that I could go to for help.

I pulled out my phone, and sent a quick text to Ian, Chris and Emily. Hoping that perhaps one of them could warn Damian. Next I dialed nine-one-one and relayed my observations to the dispatcher. She assured me that the information would be passed on to the patrols.

Putting my phone back in my jacket pocket, I debated what my next course of action had to be. I was supposed to go to the library to work on the clue, but would I be able to concentrate on anything if I was worrying about what might happen to Damian? There was definitely no way I would. I pulled my hat down tighter over my ears to ward off the biting cold, and began to run in the direction of the café.

Keeping to the main streets I wound my way into the section of town where Joanie's Café stood. It didn't take long to notice the groups of students who were roving around the area as well. They moved in small packs, three or four together, so as not to attract undue attention, but the entire group was there.

As they walked by the café, I could see them peering into the building trying to catch a glimpse of Damian. I was going to just walk in and ask to speak to Damian and give him a warning when I saw Tony Despenzo going in. There was no way to get a message to Damian without giving myself away.

I crept towards the side of the café, and stood just behind the dumpster. It gave me some shelter from the wind, kept me out of sight of the roving groups and still provided me with a decent view of the doors.

I had been standing there for only a few minutes when my phone vibrated. Carefully I pulled it out and looked at the new message from Emily. The good news was that Damian wasn't working tonight. She had overheard him tell a friend that it was his night off and he was going to the mall on the edge of town. The bad news was that the mall wasn't all that far from where I was standing right now.

I stood paralyzed. My stomach roiled with disgust wondering how the heck my fellow students could do this. How could they, in good conscious, attack one of their own classmates just because he was different? It was a question that I had no answer for at all. I knew that regardless of the answer, I would have to move if I wanted to have any chance of finding Damian before the crowd did and help him escape the growing restlessness of the mob.

Watching the door, I started to step out and then spied Tony talking to several of his regular cronies just inside. They gave each other weird hand slaps that guys often do, and then walked out into the chilly night air. I kept myself in the cover of the dumpster and let them pass.

"Yeah, the old lady at the register said that Reynolds was planning to hit the mall tonight," Tony said as he passed by me.

"Let's get the cars then and take us a trip to the mall," Tony's right hand goon, Matt Grainer, said.

I knew that I had to find Damian right now. The countdown had started, and with this group when the clock hit zero, who knew what was going to happen.

CHAPTER 5

RACE AGAINST TIME

Realizing that a fight is brewing is one thing. Realizing that you are going to be helpless to do much to help the stop the attack will set on a panic attack like no other. My mind was flying over various thoughts. How was I going to beat the mob to the mall? They had cars, and I was going to have to run. How would I ever find Damian once I was there? I was by myself, and the mob had actually shown some glimmers of intelligence back at the café by splitting up. I needed help and I needed it now.

I stopped running when the pain in my sides felt like it was going to tear me in two, and my lungs were on fire. Leaning over, trying to catch my breath, I decided to text the rest of my little group and see if I could enlist their help in this. Thirty seconds later, I was running again, hoping that I would be able to make it in time.

The mall in Sleepy Hollow is situated on the edge of the wooded park near the river. The roads all go around the park, probably in an attempt to leave the park in near pristine order. As I was approaching the river, I had an idea: if I ran through the park, my distance would be shorter and I might gain a few seconds of an advantage. Without a second thought, I turned and ran into the woods.

Knowing that there are times when it is good to work on impulse alone is okay, but I need to remind myself that there are reasons to think twice about any given action. Running into the woods of the park seemed like a good idea at first to give me a short cut to the mall, however it didn't take long for me to rethink my original idea. Unfortunately, I was doing that rethinking at the bottom of a snow covered ravine.

It seems in my haste to get to the mall, I forgot about the small creek that runs into the Hudson that was less than a half-mile in from the edge of the woods. Being as focused as I was on getting to Damian in time, I just rushed right through between the trees and suddenly found myself tumbling sideways into the ravine. I landed with a muted splash as my right shoulder and arm broke through the thin sheet of ice and plunged into the water below.

I lay there staring up at the first stars that were beginning to peek through the cloudless night fighting to get my breath back. "Whew," I said aloud, "it was lucky that I didn't end up totally in the creek."

Fighting back the nauseous feeling that was now radiating from my stomach, I rolled up onto my knees and forced myself to breathe in slow steady breaths. In and out, I kept telling myself. As the world around me stopped spinning, and my head became more aware of what was going on around me, I turned to look at where exactly I was.

I had spent time as a child running through this park, often playing in this creek while my father fished at the mouth where it emptied into the river. So I had a pretty solid working knowledge of the area, but this particular bend in the creek was unfamiliar to me. I forced myself to get up and looked around. The edge of the ravine that I had plummeted down was about ten feet high, but there was something else that was disorienting about being here.

It took a minute before I clued in to what it was. There was a glowing light that seemed to hover in the trees just across the creek. Looking around, I spotted several large rocks that had been dropped during the last retreat of the glacier that had once covered this area. Lucky for me, they were positioned in the creek bed. Scrambling up the nearest one, I was able to carefully pick my way across three of them until I was across the creek. All that was left was for me to climb up out of the ravine.

Grabbing an exposed root, I pulled myself up until I could get a grip on one of the trees that grew on the bank. After a few more strategic moves, I was out of the ravine and about ready to continue my flight to the mall to stop the mob.

Unaware of my exact location, I turned in a slow circle. I could see the lights from the houses that bordered the road to the west. My eyes again fell on the glowing light that came from the east though. Blindly, I started walking towards the light, and as I got closer, I could feel the actual temperature warming.

I stepped into a small clearing that was ringed with river rock. At the center of the circle, a floating orb hovered two feet off of the ground. "What's going on?" I asked myself. The orb began to pulse and gave off a whistling sound. My initial reaction was to take a step back, but there was something that continued to pull me to the center of the circle. "I must have really hit my head," I mumbled.

The orb transformed into a woman with long blonde hair, clothed in a regal looking silver gown. She looked at me, and though her lips didn't move, I heard her voice echoing in my head. "Descendent of Abraham Von Brunt, I have brought you here to give you a lesson."

"A lesson?" I stammered. I didn't have time for a lesson, I needed to get to the mall and warn Damian!

"You're too eager to do as you please, take it slow and find your peace. Once you do you will succeed. Take a breath, a chance to pause; you will need strength to win this cause. Be true to your allegiances and follow your heart; that is the where you should start."

"What?" I asked as the vision began to shimmer and fade out of sight. "What the heck is going on?" I screamed into the darkness.

A revving engine from the street brought me back to the immediacy of the moment. A quick check of my bearings and I was racing off again.

Thrashing through knee high underbrush, drifted snow slowed me down. It took at least twenty minutes to reach the little street that ran into the back parking lot of the mall. I slumped out into the freshly plowed area, and bent over at the waist, totally wasted from the energy that I had had to expend to get here.

The sound of an oncoming car caused me to look up. They had turned off into the first entrance, so I didn't have to avoid getting hit. "C'mon," I whispered in an attempt to motivate myself. One painful step at a time, I started making my way towards the nearest entrance.

Pulling open the huge glass doors in the entrance, I was blasted with the heat from the industrial heaters. It felt good on my frozen extremities, but I had to force myself to keep pushing on. Somewhere in this expanse of multi-level stores were two factions: Damian and the mob that wanted to kill him.

I walked through the corridors as fast as I could, looking into each glass paned storefront, hoping that I would find him first. I was on the second level when I heard the shouts. I looked over the ledge to the see the walkway below, and saw a boy I knew, Sam Kinshaw, hurdling over a bench in pursuit of something. Or more likely, someone I thought.

I made my way over to the stairs and as fast as my abused legs would carry me, headed in the same direction. Moments later, I saw what looked to be a group gathering around in the corner of the lot. "Oh, no! They must have found him," I almost screamed at a group of confused looking older women who had turned at the sounds.

Rounding the edge of the building, I kept as close to the wall as I could to stay out of view of the mob. It was clear, even from this distance that they were wailing on someone. My throat seemed to close off, and my vision blurred because of the horror that I was seeing. I had to stop this before it got out of hand, and get help here as fast as I could.

Running blindly, I pulled out my phone and again dialed nine-one-one.

"Nine-one-one, what's your emergency?" the voice of Marsha Evans, the dispatcher, said.

"This is Stevie Nixon, I'm at the Sleepy Hollow Mall, at the entrance off of Swan Street. There is a mob of people that appear to be beating someone up."

"Stevie, are you sure that someone is in trouble this time? When you called an hour ago, we sent people out looking for the person you mentioned, but nothing was found."

I gritted my teeth and fought back a scream. "Mrs. Evans, when I called an hour ago I alerted you that a mob was looking for Damian Reynolds. It appears that they found him. Please send help."

"All right, all right, hold your shirt on." I heard several clicks and what sounded like a muted radio call. Sirens echoed in the dark. "Help is on the way, Stevie. You need to stay until an officer talks to you."

"Thank you. Please have them hurry. Wait," I could see the flashing lights making the corner. "The first car just arrived."

"Take care," she said as the line went dead.

I kept making my way toward the enraged mob as the police car swerved into the lot, and flooded the area with a spot light.

The moment that the light hit the mob, they were scurrying off. Two more cars arrived, and the officers gave foot chase to some of the mob, while one officer was applying first aid to the body that was face down on the pavement.

Clenching my fists, I continued towards the circle of cop cars, afraid of what I was going to find. I was thirty feet away when I recognized Officer Rick Parrish who was performing CPR on the sprawled body. I inched closer, I could see the blood covered face that was now misshaped from the massive amount of swelling. I felt sick to my stomach, turned and leaned on the nearest car.

I heard the hard slap of shoes on the pavement coming towards me, but I didn't open my eyes.

"You okay there, miss?" a woman's voice asked.

"Not really," I managed to get out. "Is he dead? Did they kill Damian?" I asked. Another siren came in.

"He's still fighting. The ambulance just got here, so he's in good hands now." She waited a minute, and I could hear the EMTs working on Damian. I felt her hand gently pull my shoulder, "Why don't we walk over here and you can talk to me for a few minutes while they're getting your friend taken care of," she added while guiding me to the back end of the car.

"May I have your full name, for the record please?"

I swallowed and took a deep breath. I'd done everything I could to prevent this from happening, now talking to this officer was all that was left. "I'm Stevie Nixon. I called the report in."

"Okay, Stevie. Marsha told us that you would be here on scene. Can you tell me what happened?"

For the next ten minutes, I ran through almost everything that had happened starting with talking to Mr. Bigelow. The only thing that I left out was my apparent conversation with an apparition. I figured that would probably tip the scales for me from helpful-friend to crazy-girl.

As we were finishing up, I noticed a red car creeping into the lot. As soon as it was stopped, Ian and Emily were out and running towards me. When the officer I had been talking to saw them, she took a few steps back and motioned them to come to me. Ian pulled me into one of his trademarked bear hugs and just held me as the tears started to flow.

"I was too late," I sobbed.

"Stevie, hey, Stevie, it's okay. You got people to look for him and you did the best that you could. You can't be upset at yourself about this," Ian said while patting my back.

I felt a hand on my shoulder, the touch of a close friend; Emily. "He's alive right now because you fought enough to find where he was and call in the cavalry before it was too late."

"But I couldn't prevent it! Why did this happen? Damian is such a sweet, funny guy. How could anyone hate him that much?" I complained.

I let Ian lead me to the front of his car where he had me sit down. The only time that his arms left me was when he wrapped a thick wool blanket around my shoulders to help stop my shivering. Together we watched as the rescue team loaded Damian up into the ambulance. As soon as the doors were closed, the sirens began to wail and they were off in a life or death race.

Several officers came over to talk to me individually, I guessed that they were trying to gather as many facts as they could, hoping that each conversation would jog my memory some more and provide them with more details.

An hour later, the last officer left, and the three of us were alone at Ian's car. I knew that I needed to tell them about the apparition that I'd seen on my way in, but I wasn't sure of the best way to bring it up.

"Stevie," Emily said quietly, "why don't we pack it in for the night and go back to your place and try to relax a bit. You still look really freaked out."

Ian laughed, "Emily, I'd think that Stevie has a perfectly good reason to be in shock."

"Actually," I said before either of them could continue their debate over my reactions, "something else happened on the way through the woods. I'm still trying to work out what it was."

Ian spun around frantically, "What happened, Stevie?"

I told them of the apparition that I'd seen and what was said between us.

"That's cool," Emily beamed. "You've actually had contact with the ethereal plain."

"Yeah, it's wonderful, Em. Now, not only do I have to suffer through the winter of the witch, I've got to deal with poltergeist too! Enough is enough, really!"

Ian just laughed as he guided the car towards the entrance to the park. "This is about as far as we can go by car," he said. "We'll have to walk the rest of the way."

"Wonderful," I remarked.

We walked in and found the ravine that I had tumbled into earlier. "It's right over there, by those three trees that are close together. All we have to do is float over the creek and we'll be all set," I said as my teeth began chattering again.

Ian grabbed onto one of the tree trunks and swung himself part way down. Reaching his hand to me, "Grab hold, and I'll let you down to the creek bed. We'll cross over and repeat on the other side."

I shrugged my shoulders, and moments later I was standing next to the creek. Emily was at my side a second later, and then together we gave Ian a hand down. Getting across the rocks and up the other side was a bit trickier, but miraculously, we all stayed dry.

Crossing to a clearing that was now void of snow, I pointed, "This is it. She was right here when she spoke to me."

"Where were you?" Emily asked.

I scanned the area looking for my footprints. The moonlight gave just enough contrast to see where I'd stumbled earlier. "There!" I said, pointing again.

Ian looked around the point where I had been standing while Emily walked around the full circle. I watched them for a few moments and then, because I felt guilty, started looking around the clearing myself.

Ferns edged the circle, with wide leafs, but right at the point where my apparition had been, there was only dried leaves. "This makes no sense," I said. "The entire area is covered with a foot of snow, yet this one section is not only bare, but it's dry as well."

"Your apparition must have been throwing off a bit of heat," Ian said in a clinical tone.

I kicked at the leaves with my foot, and something heavy slid over the leaves. "I've got something here," I stated as I bent down to pick it up.

"What is it?" Emily asked.

"I don't know," I replied as I held out my hand with the small bronze colored medal now nestled in my palm.

CHAPTER 6

UNKNOWN MEANINGS

Snow continued to fall in the morning when I finally pulled myself from bed. I felt like I'd been run over by a fleet of trucks; every muscle in my body ached and I had bruises that covered my side where I had tumbled down the ravine.

Stepping into the bathroom, I flipped on the light. The picture here wasn't any prettier. My face showed some light bruising under my right eye. Wonderful, I thought. I didn't feel much better after the shower, but at least I was still moving under my own steam.

Downstairs, Kyle just stared at me. "What?" I asked in a snippy voice that mirrored the irritation that I felt.

"I heard what you did last night, Stevie," he said. I could hear the compassion in his voice. "I know that you didn't get there fast enough to prevent Damian from getting the stuffing beat out of him, but everyone knows that it was you who made the calls that inevitably saved his life."

"What do you mean, 'everyone knows'?" I asked.

He swallowed part of the muffin he was working on, "I got a text from Zach last night. He was at the mall when everything happened, and saw you running to help. He said that several other people noticed you as well. Personally, I think it's great to have a sister that is brave enough to do things like this." He patted my arm as he walked out.

I laid my head on the breakfast bar, and fought back the tears. "Hey, Stevie. What's wrong, Honey?" my mom asked pulling me into a hug.

"Mom, if everyone knows that I'm responsible for stopping the mob form killing Damian, that means that those who were in the mob also know. I may have just inadvertently put myself on their hit list."

"Stevie, your dad and I taught you and Kyle to always do what you thought was right; to stand up for those who needed help. You did that and more last night. We couldn't be more proud of you. We'll work through the rest of this as it comes. If you don't feel safe at any point, go to the office and we'll come get you, okay?"

"Yeah, I know that you will, but it's just I really don't need any more complications in my life right now, you know?"

She tightened her grip on me, "I know," she said. "I was also thinking that it was probably about time that we had another group meeting about the next clue." I looked up at her, wondering what I should say, but she continued before I opened my mouth. "I know that you and the others have been working on the clue, but I think that the more heads we put together on this, the better chance we have. And yes, that's *we*. Everyone here has a stake in this."

I buried my head into her breast and let the tears fall.

Walking through the halls at school that day turned out to be easier than I had feared. Many of the students, and some of the teachers, stopped me in the halls to express their support for what I had done. Mr. Bigelow even pulled me into his office and we talked about my idea for a support group again. This time, however, he had the names of two teachers who wanted to co-sponsor the group. It appeared my worrying about things was for naught, although there were still times during the day I was a little unsure of things. Like when I saw Gabby and her group, the sneers that they had on their faces made me wonder if I should make fast tracks to the office or not. I might have if it hadn't been for Mrs. Vallente who stepped in and dispersed the crowd.

At lunch, I talked to my regular group about everything. "It's been weird today, with everyone staring at me. I really didn't do that much," I protested.

"Stevie," Chris said in a solemn voice, "by finding out about what they intended to do and alerting the authorities to it and then pursuing it like you did, you most likely saved Damian's life. You showed everyone in the school, that there was someone who was willing to take a stand and support a fellow student."

"Chris is right," Ian chimed in. "People know that Damian isn't one of your close friends, but that you did what you could to help him. That makes people take notice."

I let the thought percolate for a few moments while I chewed my sandwich. "Switching gears," I said, "My mom wants everyone to come over tonight. Probably right after dinner. She'd like to have a big pow-wow about how we are doing on solving the next clue." I shook my head before I went on. "I didn't have the heart to tell her that we don't have much."

"Maybe we have more than we realize," Emily added. "Whatever, it would probably be worthwhile to get everyone involved in this and see what we can do. I'll be over around seven if that works on your end."

"That should be fine," I agreed. Ian and Chris were both consulting their phones to clear their schedules. I tried to put everything out of my mind and just concentrate on getting through the rest of the day.

Listening to my teachers for the rest of the day was an exercise in self-control. I didn't want to be at the school any longer today. There were too many thoughts that kept bouncing around in my head. I worked to keep my mind on the two major concerns that I had; finding the answer to the clue that the witch had left me, and figuring out what was going on with Chris.

Thankfully, the last bell of the day rang and I was able to make my way towards the exit.

"Gotta be feeling pretty smug about yourself?" Gabby sneered as she pushed me into the bank of lockers. "Next time you won't screw up our plans." She stomped away with her groupies laughing.

I hung my head down, and exhaled slowly. This wasn't the time for a confrontation with her, especially when I was this outnumbered.

Dinner that night with my family seemed to take forever. I had to concentrate on putting a few forkfuls of meatloaf into my mouth so that my mom wouldn't get terribly upset. I knew that I had to keep up with the impressions that everything was going normally. The reality was I was working very hard to keep myself calm, and I was afraid that one little unexpected action would send me over the edge. Thankfully, Kyle took my mind off of things relating something from school.

"It was pretty interesting in gym today," he said while shoveling mashed potatoes into his mouth. "When Tony walked in, several of the football players went over and got in his face."

"What did they do?" Mom asked.

"Nothing much," he shrugged. "They just let him know that they would not tolerate him hurting people. He knows that they know that he was one of the instigators in everything that happened to Damian."

"Good for them," my dad said. "It's good to know that people will stand up for what's right."

Just then, the doorbell rang. I glanced at the clock on the wall. I wasn't expecting anyone for another half hour. "I'll get it," I said as I pushed away from the table.

Ian stood on the other side of the glass door, holding a bouquet of flowers. Pulling the door open I greeted him, "Hi, Ian! Flowers? Is there an occasion that I didn't know about?"

His answer was a passionate kiss.

While my head was still spinning, he handed me the tied bunch of roses. "The flowers are just my way of reminding you that you are special. I picked roses, because they are hardy and grow in some of the toughest places, but they still force their way through. Because of that, they reminded me of you: a tough,

beautiful lady who does what ever it takes to make it through."
He kissed me again, and I just closed my eyes and held on tight.

I led him into the family room, "Take a seat, I'm going to go get a vase to put these in. I'll be right back."

I headed for the kitchen, which took me right past my family who were still sitting in the dining room. "Stevie," my mom gasped. "I was going to ask who was at the door, but roses? That would mean that Ian is here, right?"

I just nodded.

She got up from the table, "Let me help you find a suitable vase, and then we can all go and have dessert in the family room."

Emotions were running high an hour later as the group of us sat in our family room. Mom and dad were on the two-cushioned love seat, Kyle was sprawled in an armchair with his feet hanging over the arms, Nonni and Poppy sat on the couch along with Emily. Chris was leaning in the doorway, while Ian was in the rocker, and I sat in a chair I had dragged in from the dining room. Everyone here had concerns about where we needed to start on the clue. Unfortunately, our little meeting had also included some yelling already which had brought me to tears. No matter what happened, everyone in this room had something riding on my solving this clue.

"What we need to do is figure out how this clue relates to our past," Poppy said. "The curse came down through our family, it would make sense that somehow the answers must lie there too."

"I'm not sure about that, dad," my dad said. "While it's possible that part of the clue may come from there, what ever task it is that Stevie has to complete has to be done in the now. We need to look at what's going on today to figure out the direction."

I just listened. There were still too many opposing thoughts for me to put things together just yet. I was startled when Ian spoke up, almost as if he was in a trance.

"The answer lies somewhere between the two extremities. The clue is from the past, so the past is where we must begin. The task is from the here-and-now. What we need to do is to look at the past and see how it applies to the future, and determine what must be done now to preserve it."

When he finished speaking, every eye was trained on him. His face was blank, as if he was lost in a thought that was miles away from us.

"Ian, are you alright?" I asked, taking his hand.

It was several seconds before he blinked. "Sorry about that, I must have been lost in a deep thought." He looked around at all of us, still staring at him. "What? What happened?"

"You just gave us a tremendous insight to the problem. It was very wise," I said.

"I did?" His face went grim. "Dang! I hate when that happens!"

"You hate giving good advice or being wise?" Chris quipped.

Ian shook his head. "Neither. You're all saying that I said something that was useful, right? But the problem is, I don't have any recollection of it. I have no idea what I said."

"It looked like you were in a trance," I commented. "I just thought you were deep in thought."

He shook his head again. "Listen, what I need right now is for someone to tell me what it is that I said. I have a suspicion that a supernatural force just worked through me and gave us something we really need to use." He noticed my face. "Look, if we can believe in a curse that is two-hundred plus years old, why can't we believe in having a little spiritual intervention?"

I started to move my mouth, but no sound was coming out. Luckily, Emily found her voice and repeated what he had said.

Solving this clue was going to take time, but at least we had a good start. I ended up running up to my room twice to bring down the various clues that had been left. As I was coming down the second time, a memory flooded back. The medal that I had found in the woods near where I had had my vision on the night that Damian was attacked. I took a quick detour to the hall where my coat was hung on its peg and extracted the small charm from the inside pocket where I had tucked it away.

Returning to the family room, I dropped the written notes on the table as I passed, but kept the charm in my hand as I took my seat. While everyone else was looking over the notes, I let my memory run though what the vision had said muttering the words to myself, "You're too eager to do as you please, take it slow and find your peace. Once you do you will succeed. Take a breath, a chance to pause; you will need strength to win this cause. Be true to your allegiances and follow your heart; that is where you should start."

"What was that, Stevie?" Poppy asked.

"I'm sorry, I didn't mean to interrupt everyone's train of thought." I noticed that all conversations had stopped, and everyone was now looking at me. Taking a deep breath, I plunged ahead. "We've been looking at the written clues that have been left, but there are two other parts of the puzzle that I came across yesterday, and I just realized that we never put them on the table tonight."

I shifted uncomfortably in my chair. "Yesterday, as I was running through the woods near the mall, trying to get to Damian in time, I had a vision..." Over the next few minutes, I filled them in on the vision, and repeated the phrase that I had been told.

"Finally, as we were coming home last night, we stopped and looked in the area where I had had the vision, and we found this." I held up the little charm so everyone could see it, and then passed it for closer inspections. "I think that these two clues or hints, or whatever we want to call them, need to be added into the mix."

Accepting that we hadn't fully solved the clue tonight, we all decided it was time to call it a night around eleven. It was comforting to know that although we didn't have the solution, there were people around me who cared about me, and what happened to me. It was these same people that were working with me to ensure that I was going to come through this okay in the end.

I waved as the parade of cars left our driveway. Ian was the only non-family member who stayed behind, and now he stood behind me with his arms wrapped around my waist as we watched my grandparents head down the street. I felt his lips touch the top of my hair.

Reaching back, I rubbed the back of his neck. "I know that you can't do this for me, but knowing that you're here in my corner makes me stronger. Please, don't let go."

"It took me long enough to get you here, I'm not planning on letting you out for a long time."

He kissed me once more before he slipped on his jacket, and bid me goodnight.

As I lay in my bed, waiting for sleep to take me, my mind ran through the events of the past forty-eight hours. Subconsciously, my mind was telling me that the answer was right in front of me.

CHAPTER 7

A FRIEND IN NEED

Misty jumped onto my chest as I lay on my bed the next afternoon after school. Dropping her chew toy, she wagged her stubby tail hoping that I would take the time to play. "Not now, girl," I said scratching her head.

I had spent the day pushing my growing anxiety of the mystery of the clue out of my head. I knew that I was overlooking something important, but I just couldn't put my finger on it.

Finding out that Chris wasn't in school again today, increased the level of stress from that front. I needed to find a way to relax.

I checked my phone, for what had to be the tenth time this afternoon, to see if Chris had responded to my text from this morning. "Nothing," I mumbled as I tipped the screen towards Misty. "He didn't show up in school today, and nobody has heard from him." Misty just licked my nose and gnawed her chew toy. I closed my eyes let the thoughts continue to bounce around until Mom called me for dinner.

Everyone but Mom was already at the dinner table when I came down, following the scent of Mom's sauce. Dad was looking over the financial section of the paper and Kyle was reading a book. I dropped unceremoniously into my chair, and looked across the table at Kyle, who appeared to be finishing his homework at the dining room table. "What are reading?"

Kyle glared over the top of the book, "I've got to read *The Great Gatsby* for English. Ms. Daily called home to let Mom know that I haven't exactly been keeping up with reading it. Now I've got to sit here so Mom can watch me read while she's fixing dinner."

" I remember reading bits of that book. I can't say that it was my favorite either, but I just pushed through it." My Dad grunted and turned the page of the paper.

"Well, until I get paroled, I get to sit here and read." He glanced over his shoulder. Mom stood with her hands on her hips glaring at him. He quickly put his nose back into the book.

"Stevie," Mom called. "Would please take care of setting the table?"

I nodded and rose. As I was pulling the plates out of the cupboard, "Mom, did you get a look at the medallion that I found the other night?"

"Yes. Why do you ask?"

"I think that there is a relation between the figures on it and the clue that I found on the winter solstice. It just seems to be eluding me right now."

"Hmmm. You may very well be right. We'll take another look after dinner."

As I was setting the plates, I thought about how different things were this time around. When I was faced with the first clue, I went about solving it primarily by myself with help from my close friends. This time, I've got my family involved. I'm still scared of the outcome, but I feel better knowing that everyone is behind me.

Conversations over dinner in our house typically ran the gamut. We'd talk about how each of our days had been and then drift into a topic that was timely. Today it was the quest that Dad decided that we should talk about. "Have you had any luck with breaking the hieroglyphics from the clue yet?" he asked.

"No. Not Yet. I was telling Mom, that I think that there must be a link between the clue itself and the medallion. I'm pretty sure that the same series of symbols is on both."

"I've got a thought," Kyle interjected. "When we were discussing things last night, you said that the last clue had been given to you in Latin and that once you translated it, you still had to put it into an acrostic. What if this is giving you the letters, and you need to figure out what they stand for."

I could feel the blood draining out of my face. "What do you mean, Kyle?"

"For example, we all know that T.G.I.F. is Thank Goodness It's Friday, right? What if it's like that?"

"That still doesn't help with figuring out what the letters are." I sat there with a fork full of pasta, just staring out into space. The ringing of the telephone jolted me back to reality.

"No, Joyce. He's not here. Let me ask Stevie." Mom turned holding her hand over the mouthpiece. "It's Chris' mom. Have you seen him today?"

"No," I replied as I swallowed quickly. "I was worried about him today when he wasn't in school. I texted him, but he never responded."

Mom relayed the information to Mrs. Lehr-Brown and my mind started to get real antsy. Something was really wrong now.

Mom came back to the table, "She sounds really worried about Chris. Apparently he and Mark got into another round last night. She hasn't seen him since."

"She didn't find it strange that he wasn't in bed last night?" my dad asked.

"Joyce said that when she went up, she could hear Chris tossing in bed. When they got up this morning, there was a note on the table saying that he'd forgotten to tell them that he was meeting with one of the teachers before school to get some extra help. When he wasn't home when they got this evening, Joyce assumed that he'd come over here."

"Mom," I said softly, "I need to be excused now. Suddenly I'm not hungry."

"Honey, do you know anything about where Chris might be?"

"I wish I did. He's had so much on his plate right now he hasn't even been acting like himself for the last few weeks. We've all been worried about him."

"Have you tried to talk to him about it?" Dad asked.

"Yeah. I met up with him the other day. He just said that he and Mr. Brown had been having some major disagreements. I know that he—" I broke off for a minute. Chris had told me about the therapist, but was that in confidence? "He and Mr. Brown have been working with someone to resolve things."

Silence hung in the air for what seemed an eternity. "Mom? Please? I need to see if I can find him."

"Take your phone, and use my car. Be careful, Honey. Good luck."

With her blessing, I ran out the back door hoping that Chris was okay.

Leaving the house, I had to force myself to slow down. It would be too easy to just race off in some, any, direction. "Take your time and think this through," I said to myself, my voice coming out in little wisps of vapor. Turning towards town, "Where did Chris like to go when we just wanted to go somewhere to hang out?" I asked the night.

As I neared the town, I started to get some definite ideas. When we had been in eighth grade, we had all gone into the park near the mall, and headed up the side of the big hill. We'd made a fire up at the top and had a grand old time. But that had been in the summer when the temperature was near eighty-five, not a February night when it was three degrees out with two feet of snow.

Instinctively, I turned away from there. There were some hiking trails that we liked to use. Again, I doubted that he would go that way.

I was almost to the other side of the village, when inspiration hit. I pulled over and yanked out the phone. "Mom, I think I know where Chris is."

Swinging the car into the marina down by the river, I looked around for any signs that Chris had been here. My mind went back to the year that Joyce had met Mark. Chris had felt out of place, so we had been spending lots of time goofing off together. We had ridden our bikes down here one day, and had found an old abandoned cabin that had been overgrown in the woods.

We'd never had any idea when the cabin had been put here, but it's owner had long since deserted it. We ended up making several trips there over that summer. And from talking with Chris over the next few years, it became apparent that he would visit the cabin once or twice a year, claiming that it was a good place to think.

I pushed out of the car, and headed for the underbrush. As I neared the edge where the trail was, I noticed several different footprints. "It's not a guarantee, but it sure looks right."

Fifteen minutes later, I recognized the old train trestle that spanned the inlet. I smelled smoke from a wood fire, and felt my heart surge ahead. Turning left, I followed the shore and saw a light beaming through a broken window.

I walked to the broken down building and peered in the window. Chris lay on the floor wrapped in what appeared to be an old sleeping bag in front of the fire. I knocked on the door, and I could see his head jerk around.

There were stains on his cheeks from the most recent round of crying. My heart broke. "Chris? It's me, Stevie. Can I come in?"

I heard the scraping of something heavy being moved from in front of the door. A lone train whistle pierced the night. The door swung open and I looked at my friend who seemed to have aged fifteen years overnight.

"Chris, what's going on?" I rushed through the door and gave him a hug. I felt his shoulders shaking and his tears on my neck. Surveying the room, I saw nothing that was out of the ordinary apart from his gear. His ancient backpack leaned against the wall, his sleeping bag and... "Chris, why do you have a shot gun here?"

Pushing the door closed, I led Chris back to the fire where we could sit on the sleeping bag and still be somewhat warm. Rubbing his hands with mine, I just sat there and tried to comfort him through the tears. It took nearly ten minutes for him to cry himself out. I handed him a few tissues that I had in my pocket.

"Thanks. Oh God, Stevie, how did things go so wrong?"

"Hey, it's alright now," I said rubbing his back. "What's going on, and don't feed me a line of bull, okay? I just hauled myself through the woods and snow to find you. Tell me what's eating you."

His head hung lower than it had been. "I'm not sure I can. I mean, I really want to tell you, but I don't know how."

"Start at the beginning. And perhaps it will just start flowing from there. What caused all of this?" I motioned around the room.

He took a deep breath. "I came here today to kill myself, Stevie."

My throat closed up. "What? Why would you do that?" I stammered. I could hear my heart hammering on my rib cage, while tears began streaming down my cheeks.

"I'm not sure I can face the truth any more. I'm different, Stevie. Everyone knows it. Recent events have only reinforced things. I just figured that it would be better for everyone if I didn't exist, so I'd planned to end it all."

"Oh, Chris. Is this all because of the fight with Mark last night?"

"The fight was the final push. I just can't take any more of him putting me down, slapping at me—"

"He hit you?" I nearly shrieked.

"No, but he's constantly beating me up verbally, you know? I told him last night that I needed to take the next step. My therapist and I agreed that this is what I needed to do, and he went ballistic. He started calling me every derogatory name he could think of. It ended when I tried to walk out of the room and he grabbed my shirt and it tore. When he saw how devel…" his voice trailed off.

"Chris," I asked tentatively, "What's wrong. Is this still having to do with the drugs you were caught ordering?"

He looked me in the eye, "Yeah, it is. I have a big problem."

"Knowing that you have been ordering pills on-line for a while is a problem for all of us. But there is something else going on here. Let me help you, Chris. You've been one of my closest friends since elementary school. I can't lose you."

He shrugged, looked around the cabin and sighed. "Stevie, I," he hesitated. "I've always felt that my body and mind didn't match."

"We all have issues with our bodies. We're teenagers, Hon." I smiled, hoping that it would reassure him.

"That's not what I'm talking about." He shook his head and stared at the ceiling as if waiting for the words to come down. "Stevie, I've always felt like I was in the wrong body. You know that I've always hung out with you and Emily; I enjoy sewing and other crafts. I really think I should have been…" He swallowed hard. "I think I should have been born a girl."

To say that I was shocked would be an understatement. "What do you mean? How long have you felt this way?"

"My first memory of feeling like this was when I was about three, or so. I really don't ever remember *not* feeling like this. I tried to fight it; I played sports. Or at least I attempted to play. I hoped that I'd grow out of it, but it's only gotten worse. Three years ago, I saw a show on T.V. about boys who want to become girls. I did some research, and found out the basic treatment was therapy and to use cross hormones to change the body."

"I couldn't get into therapy without telling my mom, but I found that I could order the pills online. At first, nothing happened, so I kept taking them. At the end of the summer, just before our junior year, I noticed that my chest felt tingly. By Christmas, I had the start of breasts, almost to the point that they were noticeable through my shirts. That's when I started wearing the real baggy clothes and let my hair grow."

"Mark didn't like the clothes or the hair, but didn't say much other than I needed a hair cut. Everything seemed to be going fine until just before school got out. By then I'd developed about a B cup, so I had to bind them to keep them from being seen. Anyway, last May, I'd gotten home early from school, Mom wasn't due home for nearly two hours, Mark was out of town and it was so hot that I'd taken off my outer shirt, and removed the binding. I was sitting at the computer in my room wearing a tank top and jeans when my mom walked in. Let's just say there was no where to hide anything."

"She and I sat on my bed, me in tears and her ready to spit nails, and I gave her the whole story. She agreed to get me into counseling, and I was to stop the meds. Well the counselor diagnosed me fairly quickly as having a condition called Gender Dysphoria. What it means is that I'm transgendered, likely even transsexual. He recommended that I resume the medications under his direction. Mom was not happy, but things moved forward."

"And then Mark found out just after school began this year. He went off on a rampage that sent me to my room shaking. He cut off the meds, and went on a super push to make a man out of me. I need to be a woman, so I needed my meds. If he wouldn't let me use the prescriptions from the doctor at the pharmacy, I decided that I'd use them and order on-line."

"He found out again over Christmas that I'd been getting the meds. So, Mom took me to another shrink, and we got the same diagnosis. This time, she is forcing Mark to let me have the meds and he's just going ballistic."

Chris looked at me now, "That's it. My biggest secret is out of the bag. Last night when Mark tore my shirt, he discovered that I've kept developing. Now I have a C-cup and a girlish figure to match. His decree last night was that if I want to be a girl so bad, that I'm going to start attending school as one." His eyes were vacant now. "I need to be who I am. But I don't think that I can live through that. When the mob killed that other kid and then our own classmates went after Damian, I realized that if anyone found out about me before graduation, I'd be dead."

I reached out to him, and took his hand. "Oh, Chris. I'm not sure what to say."

He laughed lightly, "Most people just want to run, or they say that I'm a freak; unnatural."

"Can I ask a few questions?"

"You know my deepest secret. The rest is just decoration."

"Why do you want to be a girl? Why can't you be a boy?

His head snapped towards me, a grin on his face. "Why can't you be a boy? Why do you want to be a girl?" he challenged.

"I was born this way."

"Me too. I don't want to be like this, I'd much rather be normal but this is the hand I've been dealt. From what my doctors said, and stuff I found on line, no one knows why this occurs. But, studies have shown that a trans-person's brain matches the brain of the gender we identify with. So, if we were to compare our brains, they would have the same shaped structures and be roughly the same size. The numbers of neurons would be the same as well."

"Wouldn't that be true for everyone?" I asked.

"Research has shown that males and females brains have distinct differences. Even though I was born a male, my brain is that of a female."

"So, you're just trying to make everything match? Right?"

"Pretty much. No one would choose to go through this. Like everyone else, I just want my brain and my body to match; to have the right parts. The only one that I can fix is my body."

"Were you ever going to tell Emily and I?"

"I'd planned to transition right after graduation. It's one of the steps that I'll need to take; living as a woman for an extended period of time. I'd really hoped to be out of here before everything came out. Anyway, I've been working on a letter that would help me explain everything, getting together a packet that has links to the pertinent web sites and some other relevant material. You two have been my best friends forever. I was hoping that I'd be able to keep you through all of this."

"I'll be here for you, Chris." We sat in silence for a few minutes, each lost in our own thoughts.

"I thought I'd be mortified to tell anyone about this. But I'm glad that you know now."

"Thanks. We probably should think about heading home. Your Mom is worried sick about you."

"She may be, but I don't know about Mark."

"Come on," I said standing up. "Let's go back to the car and go home. You can call and talk to your mom, and if need be you can crash at my place tonight."

Forty minutes later, we had packed up everything and hiked out to the car. I reached into my pocket pulling out the keys and my phone. "Give her a call," I said.

I stowed his stuff in the car while he talked and cried with his mom. When he walked back over still wiping the tears I asked, "Everything all right?"

"Yeah, I can go home. She and Mark have talked, and my therapist even came over. Hopefully things will be okay now. Thanks."

"Hey, what are best friends for anyway? By the way, what name do you use?"

He smiled. "I want to keep things as simple as possible. I like Christine, or Chrissy.

CHAPTER 8

SHAKY

Squinting through the slits of my eyes, I tried to read the clock on my desk. Two-forty-three in the morning. So far the night had proven to be a challenge to sleep through. Instead of flipping on the little light on my nightstand, I just stared at the early morning sky. Orion was just setting in the western part of the sky, and here I was wide-awake.

I wasn't exactly surprised that I wasn't sleeping after finding out about Chris, or should I now say Chrissy? I had expected something along these lines when I had researched about the hormones. But suspecting something and having it confirmed as true are two completely different experiences.

I pulled an extra blanket from the foot of my bed, and wrapped it around my shoulders. Hoping that the chill that I was feeling was simply from the night air. Of course, the way my luck was going that wouldn't be the case.

Still shivering, I tossed the blankets back and plodded over to my closet and pulled a heavy sweater off of the shelf. Pulling my legs up under myself, I curled up in the window seat and stared at the stars. Nights like these always make me wonder what the fates have in store for me.

My mind flashed over to Chris. Now that I knew what he had been hiding for all these years, when I looked back, the evidence was all too obvious. I, like almost everyone else, had seen the little pieces but had never put the puzzle together.

"Put the puzzle together," I muttered. Misty lifted her head at the sound, yawned and jumped up to cuddle with me in the window.

I shifted enough so that I could pull the clues from my desk. I looked at the first clue, the one that I had already solved. I had been totally stymied at first, but then it was by pure chance that I discovered that the clue had indeed been an acrostic poem. Carefully, I pulled out the crest that I had found during the first task. It was a picture of a duck in the middle of a spiral.

The second clue was nowhere near as long. It consisted of only five symbols and five letters. I looked again at the line of text, $\Lambda o\psi\alpha\lambda\iota\tau\varepsilon\iota\tau$, hoping that something would jump out at me.

I fingered the medal and looked at it again. The same characters were inscribed along the top. A hound with a blue stone for an eye stood in the center of a spiral with a flower in its mouth.

Setting all four items out, I began to look for the connection that had to be there. I was sure of it! Something had to bring these items together in the greater puzzle. I lost myself in thought as I fixated on the blue stone.

I jumped when the hand clasped me on my shoulder, "What the heck?" I nearly shouted in surprise.

"It's okay, Stevie. How come you're not in bed?" Dad asked.

"I couldn't sleep. My mind has been thinking about so much these last few days, and the stuff with, well, you know, with Chris. It just really jumbled everything up."

Dad sat in my desk chair. "I know that you were very reluctant to give out any details when you got home tonight, but is there anything you want to tell me about what's going on with Chris?"

"It's really personal, Dad, so it's not my place to tell." I sighed, and debated with myself if I could tell some, but not give away the secret. It's not that I can't keep a secret, but this one was causing me to lose sleep. Maybe if I shared the burden, however little, it would help. "You know that Mark and Chris haven't seen eye-to-eye for quite some time, but I found out the reason why. Chris has a medical issue that requires a treatment that Mark doesn't approve of."

"I can't see anyone getting upset about a medical treatment." He paused for a moment, "On second thought, Chris has often seemed depressed, and some of the prescriptions that they use for treating that have caused some severe side-effects. I guess I could see him getting upset. Is that what this is all about?"

Close enough I thought. "It's along those lines. The pills that Chris was taking did cause a series of reactions. Mark wants him off of the meds, but Joyce and Chris are fighting to keep him on because of how much they have helped the underlying problem."

Dad nodded his head. "Okay. Well, Chris' problem is not going to be solved by you at three in the morning. So, why don't we turn out the lights and go back to bed?"

"Sure." I stood and moved everything back to my desk.

Pointing at the small pile, Dad asked, "Having any luck with that?"

"Not really. I'm fairly sure that there is a connection, but it's alluding me."

He pulled me in close, and squeezed me tight. "I don't want you to worry about this, Stevie. We're all going to pull things together and we will figure this out in no time." He waited for me to crawl back into bed, and pulled my covers up over my shoulders. "I used to tuck you in like this every night when you were a little girl. Sleep tight, *mia figlia*."

I lay in the dark waiting for sleep to come, but I still felt restless. A cold nose on the bottom of my foot was cause for a yelp. "C'mon, Misty, get up here," I patted the cover next to me. She cuddled against my side, the warmth from her fur warming me. I eased into sleep, lulled by Misty's constant soft snores.

Dreams phased in my mind; a wooded ravine, a small cabin, running through unfamiliar area. Everything seemed so jumbled. I felt Misty move at one point, and can only guess that either my muttering or my tossing had woken her. In either case, her response was to lick my face and curl up again.

Eventually I lapsed into a deep sleep. This time the dreams that came were smooth and steady, but still unfamiliar.

I was walking through a part of the woods that are near the school. I could see the big rock where the last task had been completed. A woman was there, not someone that I knew but someone that I had seen before. On the ground at her feet, crystals were strewn in a pattern and she chanted in some strange language.

As I neared her, she smiled at me. Not a pleasant, 'come here' smile, but more of a 'finally you're here' smile. It disconcerted me but I kept inching my way forward. She threw her arms into the sky, and her fingertips began to emit a blue light. Five blots of lightening flashed from the clear sky and left smoldering splotches around her. The strewn crystals were now glowing, and it sounded as if they were humming.

As I glanced over my shoulder, the fog rolled in diminishing my vision, cutting off my escape route. Turning back to the witch, for now I knew that is who she was, I felt the cold of the night at my back. "What do you want from me?" I yelled.

Her eyes settled on me and held me in place. "What do I want?" she snarled. "'Tis ye who must find what ye seek, stand tall; protect the meek. For when you chose to let it go, ye lose everything, especially your soul." A flash of light shot from her hand, and hit me like a shot in the chest. When I gasped from the pain, she beckoned, "Step into my circle and give yourself to..."

"This is not the way!" a male voice cried out over the sounds of approaching hooves. I turned my head towards the oncoming sounds.

"My own flesh and blood would work against me?" the witch asked. Flicking her right hand towards the unseen rider, a bolt of lightening erupted from her fingertips and was answered with a cry of pain.

"Killing them makes you no better than he who caused this curse. I urge you, cousin, take the higher road. The road of honor, the road of freedom." As he finished speaking, he broke through the lingering fog.

Garbed in a cloak as black as the night, a hood pulled down obscuring his face, he sat stoically in the saddle. His mount was a broad chestnut colored horse with a white hourglass on his nose his only marking.

He reached a hand out towards me, "Come with me, my lass. Let's get you away before she damns all of us."

With no hesitation, I walked towards the hooded figure. Grasping my arm, he pulled me onto the horse. We turned and with a slight nudge of his boots, the horse galloped away. The mist faded as we neared the edge of the woods. With a "Hup," the horse leapt into the air to cross the stream at the edge.

I felt my stomach falling, and then I woke up, tangled in my sheets and blankets. Misty stood, growling towards the window her back pressed against me. I gasped for breath, and felt a searing pain run through my ribs as if I had been hit.

Running my hand under my pajama top, I felt the welts. Where the heck had I been?

Pulling my seldom-used diary from its place in my nightstand, I wrote out everything that I could remember from the dream. Something told me that I was going to need that information.

Gray clouds were just becoming visible when I finished writing out the details of the dream. I leaned back against the wall and tried to stretch out my back. Unfortunately, Misty realized that my hands were free and decided that this would be a good time for me to be petting her. She leaped up onto my chest, driving my head into the wall with a solid THUD. "Ow! Are you trying to kill me, Misty?" She only answered with a playful yip.

I don't know how long we sat there, me petting her back as she curled up with her head on my shoulder. When I glanced over at the window, there was light beginning to filter through. A check of the clock confirmed that it was really time to get moving for the day.

Stumbling into the bathroom I flipped on the light and let out a small shriek of horror. My reflection staring back at me from the mirror looked more like the bride of Frankenstein than normal. I leaned in closer; my hair was disheveled and knotted in places. It definitely looked windblown. It looked as if I had raced through the night on a horse. Lines that had never before appeared on my face, were outlined in smudges of dirt.

I looked at my hands. In the dimness of my room, I hadn't picked up the dirt that seemed to be embedded into the skin and under the nails. I hesitantly opened my robe and took off my pajamas: there was no denying the three-inch bruise that sat just under my left breast.

"What the heck?" I muttered to myself. Tenderly pressing on the bruise I winced in pain. "I look like someone who had actually been through what I saw in my dream last night. I looked only for another moment, and then carefully climbed into the shower, hoping to erase the evidence.

Most girls in my class use makeup religiously. Aside from lip-gloss, and the occasional blush, I personally found it to be too much work and effort. But I decided that today was the exception: I needed something that would help me conceal the scratches and small cuts that had appeared from under the layer of dirt that washed off in the shower.

I studied my face in the mirror in my room, and deemed that it was as good as it was going to get. Throwing the small cases into my backpack, so I could make repairs during the day, I grunted at Misty. "Well, this should be interesting. Let's go. Downstairs." She leapt off the bed and raced down the stairs while I forced myself to go down.

"Hey," Kyle smirked as I walked into the kitchen. "I didn't realize that it was dress like a clown day today."

Mom, who had been pulling out the eggs, shot up from behind the door of the refrigerator. "What do mean, dressed like a clown?" She eyed me carefully. "Stevie, your makeup looks very nice this morning. You know, many women like wearing it; it makes us feel feminine and sexy."

I rolled my eyes, just what I needed my mom to think; I was trying to look sexy. "I know Mom, I just thought I'd slap some gunk on, you know?"

"And here I thought it was in honor of it being Valentine's Day and you were trying to impress Ian."

Kyle's laugh caused him to snort out Corn Pops. It only grew worse when he saw my face.

"Valentine's Day," I repeated. "Oh blasted all! I forgot all about it. What am I supposed to do? I've never had a boyfriend before! Is there some type of protocol?" I was hitting full stride for a hysterical anxiety attack. Mom's hand gripped my shoulder and her soft voice kept from really going off the deep end.

"Stevie, take a breath. There is no specific protocol. The idea is to find a way to celebrate your love for someone. Often times you just exchange cards and candy." She was looking at me carefully. "There is something else that is troubling you, isn't there? Why don't you spill while I make you an omelet for breakfast?

Over the smell of bacon and a three-cheese omelet, I told her the basics of the dream. I wasn't going to say anything else, but I moved just right and winced.

"Are you okay, Sweetheart?" Mom asked.

"Yeah. It's just that," I rubbed my hands over the big bruise on my chest and winced again.

Before I could react, she had grabbed the shirt and yanked it up far enough that she could see. "Mercy, Stevie. What happened here?" she demanded.

"Mom, I wish I knew. It wasn't there yesterday, but when I woke this morning, it was."

She looked confused, and I could tell that she wanted to ask me something. "I can see the question in there, Mom. Ask it."

"Is this where you saw yourself getting hit in the dream?"

"I wouldn't say I saw myself. I saw everything from my own perspective. I mean, I was me. When I was hit in the dream, I saw the bolt come at me and, yes, it hit there."

She stared at me for a moment. "I normally don't believe in paranormal events, but this is really making me rethink that now. Be careful." She pulled me in for a hug, but was careful not to hurt me any further.

Seeing Emily waiting for me at the bus stop ended up being the highlight of the morning. "Have I got a tale for you," I started off.

"Think mine may top yours," she said smugly.

"Okay, go for it."

"Well, I was talking with Dee O'Brien last night. It had to be around ten or so. Anyways, we were discussing some things that she had seen around her house. It seems that there were strange lights that were pulsing from somewhere in the middle of the woods that border her place. She was kind of freaked out by them. After we hung up, I crashed and had the weirdest dream. I was kind of floating over those woods that she described. I saw the lights that we had talked about, and as I flew nearer, I saw a woman standing in a pentagram chanting. When I realized what it was, I got frightened and fought to get away. I ended up going through a snow squall."

She looked around cautiously to make sure unwanted ears weren't trying to overhear. "When I woke up in my bed, I was wet and there were still snow flakes on my hair. It was freaking weird."

"This is getting crazy," I said. Taking her hand and holding on to help keep me steady, I told her of my dream, and the resulting injuries.

"This doesn't make any sense," she said as we were boarding the bus. "If she wants you to pay for the sins of your ancestors, you would think that she would want you to succeed."

"The rider who pulled me out said that she would damn us all if she killed me outside of the curse."

"Honey, you've got things coming at you from all sides now."

"Yeah.   Curses, ghosts and psychos, oh my!   Does everything end with my death?"

CHAPTER 9

VALENTINE'S DAY

Red paper hearts covered the windows and many of the lockers in the school. As I walked towards my locker I noticed many of the other girls holding bouquets of colored flowers and candy hearts. In my rush this morning, I had been lucky enough to come by a bag of conversation hearts that Mom had stashed in the cupboards.

Turning the corner, I spied good ole Gabby surrounded by three guys. As I passed, I could hear them each vying for her to accompany them to the upcoming dance. My mind wandered, I'd seen the poster for the dance, but as of yet, Ian hadn't asked me. Should I be upset? Worried?

The hand that tapped me on my shoulder made me jump. Spinning around, I found myself face-to-face with Chris.

"Hey, Stevie," he said shyly.

"Hi." I took a good look at him. There was something different, but I couldn't see it right away. Then it hit me. "You look pretty happy today. What's happened?"

We continued walking towards my locker as he filled me in about how both his mom and Mark had been worried about him. They were going, all of them, to see the shrink tonight, and they felt pretty confident that they would be able to work things out.

By the time that I arrived in homeroom, my thoughts of the dance were getting foggy as I thought about how long it had been since I had seen Chris have a real smile on his face.

Lost in my own little world, I took my seat and didn't hear Mrs. Vallente call my name. It wasn't until the girl who sits behind me poked me with her pencil. "What?" I spun around, and she merely pointed at Mrs. Vallente who was looking at me with a puzzled expression holding out a sheet of paper.

"A little lost in the day, Ms. Nixon?"

"I'm sorry, Mrs. Vallente. I've just had a lot on my mind the last few days, and several things are coming to a head right now." Taking the sheet, I returned to my seat and looked at it.

I'm not sure which emotion hit first: elation or frustration. The note gave me a time that I was to report to Mrs. Lerch's office. I had been desperate to see her a few days ago, but so many things had changed. We had been too late for Damian, but now with the new knowledge of Chrissy, I was more determined that we needed to get some kind of protection for people.

I pulled out my phone, knowing that it wasn't really allowed during the school day. Technically the day hadn't started yet and it was on vibrate. I quickly logged in my appointment on the calendar with a reminder set for five minutes before. Hopefully I would remember what it was for when it went off.

Classes were dragging by. It was almost as if every teacher knew that I had to keep an eye on the time, because all of our activities were so short, that there was no way to get lost in doing something. All that this succeeded in doing was making me so nervous that I could no longer sit still in my seat. Every few seconds it seemed that I would fidget and look over at the wall clock or trying to get a glimpse at the watch of the person next to me. In either case, I figured that if I didn't find a way to relax I'd be a blob of goo by the time I got in to see Mrs. Lerch.

Ian smiled at me when I dropped onto my stool in Physics. He slid a folded piece of paper over to me, "Happy Valentine' Day, Stevie."

Well, that did it. I'd hit my emotional limit for the day, and broke into nearly hysterical tears. I really did feel bad for Ian, who bravely fought his instincts of running away from the hysterical female and edged closer and wrapped me in his arms.

"It's okay," he said soothingly. "I can get a better card if that's what you want."

I shook my head. "That's not it, Ian. It's not the card. Thanks by the way." I sniffled and used the sleeve of my sweater to wipe away the tears.

His hand traced out small circles on my back, "Can you tell me what I did?"

I turned quickly and caught his cheeks in my hands, and pulled him to me for a quick, passionate kiss. "You gave me a card on Valentine's Day. That's the fist time that that has ever happened. But that's not the reason for the tears. I've got to go see Lerch about the whole mob thing. So that all adds to the stress about everything else."

"It'll work out. Relax." His kissed my forehead, and kept me talking about the lab we were supposed to be working on until it was time for me to go. He gave me a quick peck for good luck and winked as I headed out the door.

Mrs. Croft smiled at me as I walked into the office a few minutes early. Shuffling the papers from her right hand to her left, she picked up the phone on her desk, "Mrs. Lerch, Ms. Nixon is here. Okay." Hanging up she motioned me towards the chairs against the wall. "Just have a seat, Deary, and Mrs. Lerch will be with you in a moment. I'd offer you a cup of coffee, but right now you look too jumpy as it is."

I smiled weakly as I took the chair closest to the office door. My eyes scanned the room and my legs trembled. "This is stupid," I muttered under my breath.

Mrs. Croft looked up, "I'm sorry, did you say something?"

Embarrassed, "I'm sorry. I was just telling myself that it was stupid to be nervous to talk to the principal. I guess I'm just wired, and I suppose concerned would also be a good adjective to use here now."

She smiled at me, "Relax, Honey. Mrs. Lerch knows that you tried to see her before the big-to-do with Damian. Mr. Bigelow has been down here and told her about your desire to start that group. I think today is more a formality and a chance to get the ball rolling."

As she finished, the door opened and Mrs. Lerch appeared. "Stevie, please, come in."

Mrs. Lerch led me into her office and motioned me to one of the chairs that flanked her desk. Sitting across from me she began, "Stevie, it has come to my attention that a few days ago you came in and expressed interest in forming a support group for students who were, um, let's say different. You then voiced your concern about a mob, made primarily of students from Sleepy Hollow High. When you were unable to resolve enough of the issue here, you tried to locate the student that they were after to warn him of the impending attack. Even though you were not able to prevent it, you were able to get medical attention for him."

She shuffled two papers on her desk, "When we inquired this morning, Damian is stable and recovering, thanks to you and your actions. When I met with Mr. Bigelow upon my return, he related the events to me, he also relayed that he had several teachers who had approached him with offers to be the faculty advisors. I have met with each of those teachers, and through mutual agreement, Mrs. Vallente has been appointed as the advisor. Now the only thing that is missing is the student membership."

"Mrs. Lerch, with the number of people who were outraged at what happened to Damian, I think that the right words by the right person and this group would have plenty of members."

"I agree. So, when would you like to address your classmates about the formation of the Sleepy Hollow High PFLAG group?"

Excuse me?" I choked. "You want me to address the student body about this? I'm not sure that I can. I mean, I'm no good at public speaking."

She leaned back in her chair and gave me that look, the one that makes all of your bones de-calcify. She waited for what seemed an hour, but was more likely only a minute or so. "Stevie, why did you come here in the first place?"

That question threw me for a loop. "Um, I was concerned about the safety of one of our students. I was abhorred that members of my school could be so uncaring about one of our own. I guess I was also worried about..." I paused. I couldn't tell her about Chrissy. That information was confidential.

"You were worried about Chris Lehr, right?"

I gulped. "Yes," squeaked out. "How did you know?"

She smiled, "I could say that it was my job to know, but that would be a lie. Actually Mrs. Brown called me this morning and gave me the run down. I now know about Chrissy, and her condition. I feel that I can discuss this with you because I was told that Chrissy told you."

A weight had been lifted off of my chest, and I exhaled in a gust. "Yeah. Yeah, she told me last night." Lifting my head, I looked into Mrs. Lerch's eyes. "I'd like to speak with Mrs. Vallente to set things up."

It took us a few more minutes to finalize a basic plan that we would work from and finish our meeting. I left her office and nearly slid down the wall, completely overwhelmed at what was happening. I needed to get away from reality for a little while.

Closing my eyes, I let myself sink to the floor in the alcove off of the hall just down from the bathrooms. My head fell back against the cold tile wall and I just closed my mind off to any sounds that were emanating from within. My head still felt mushy, like I was trying to force a coherent thought out after a long night. I just kept thinking about being above the clouds; the perfect place to escape reality for me. I could almost sense the speed as I imagined going through the puffy white cloud when a smell intruded on my daydream. It was lilacs and something else. "What the heck?" I mumbled

"Are you awake yet, or are you still in your own little world?" Ian asked.

My eyes shot open. "What are you doing here?"

"Oh, I had a delivery that required me to come to the office to pick up. When I left, I saw you here in the hall and was debating whether to wake you or call the nurse."

I glared at him, trying for a scornful look, but when he started laughing, I couldn't keep up with it and joined in. "I just finished up with Mrs. Lerch, and I felt so drained I needed a rest." My eyes flickered to the bouquet of flowers that he held in his hand. "Who are the flowers from? Your secret admirer?"

He blushed, "These are for you. I was in a hurry to get out this morning and left them in a vase in the refrigerator. My Mom brought them in on her way into work." He knelt down and held the flowers out to me.

Taking the flowers in my right hand, I pulled him in closer with my left. "Thank you, Ian. I love you, more than I can tell you. These are beautiful. I'll never forget the first Valentine bouquet that I received." The kiss that I planted on him wasn't intended to be a deep passionate kiss, but when the heat reached my toes, I gave up and just went with it.

Emotions flooded through me and the waterworks began, again. I felt myself being hoisted off of the floor, and embraced. "I wish you would trust me with whatever is bothering you so much," Ian said.

Taking a deep breath, "Ian, I'm just overwhelmed. This is the first Valentines Day where I've had someone special to share it with. Couple that with what is going on with this stupid curse, and everything with Chrissy, and then Mrs. Lerch wants me to head a chapter of PFLAG. It's just a bit too much to handle."

"Chrissy?"

"Oh, blast!" the tears began to come faster. "Please don't say anything. In fact, forget that I even said it! Oh, how could I be so stupid and careless?"

I felt his lips kiss the top of my hair. "Stevie, you're not careless. It's a situation where you have too much going on up here," he said tapping my head. "Apparently you have learned more about what is going on with our friend. When the time is right, just remember that we are here for both of you."

I leaned back and looked at him through tear stained eyes. How could he always be so calm, and so much of what I need?

I rushed home after school that night, and instead of going into the house, I detoured back to my shop. As I unlocked the door, and eased my way in, I thought back to my birthday last year when Poppy had given me the plans and materials to build my own airplane. At first, I was overwhelmed by them too, but after we went to the seminar and I studied the plans, I realized that while building a plane is a huge undertaking, it really is a matter of a series of simple, logical steps taken in order.

I walked over to where the fuselage of my little Sonex sat on saw horses waiting for the landing gear to be installed, and ran my hand over the chilly aluminum. It was smooth and strong, yet I knew that on its own it was flexible and could be bent into many shapes. Was this a metaphor of my life? I was weak and malleable, but with a little support I was able to support many things and be strong when I needed.

I flipped on the radio and studied my plans. I knew that I needed to spend a little time with my true love here. I almost always lost track of time out here and any worries that I had when I walked in disappeared as I concentrated on the plane. I didn't even hear the door when Ian let himself in ninety minutes later.

Ian hadn't told me what he was planning for celebrating tonight; I only knew that he had cleared it with my family to take me out to dinner. He was patient while I spent forty-five minutes fussing with the mess of curls that picked today to be at their orneriest, and took my time with the make-up. As I walked through the kitchen, I was pleased to see him go mute when he saw me. Apparently the time was well spent. After Mom snapped a few pictures, she wished us a good time and we were off.

I had never seen Ian wearing a suit before, and I was truly impressed with the way that he filled it out. The blue in his tie made his already potent eyes even more so. His hair, normally in a ponytail was pulled back into a very sophisticated braid.

"So, where are we going tonight?" I asked.

"What? You think we're going somewhere special? I just figured we'd hit the drive through at McDonald's," he retorted with his trademarked grin. I just reached over and gave him a playful tap.

When we pulled up at the marina, I looked over at him in surprise. "Why are we here? The restaurant here only operates during the summer."

"That's true, but we're not going to the restaurant. We're going over there," he said
pointing to the lights of a sailing vessel.

"Ah, Ian, what's going on here?"

"You're not afraid of boats are you?" Now there was a concern in his voice.

"Not exactly, but where are you planning on sailing to?"

"I'm not the one sailing," he smiled as he led me up the gangplank. "Morris," he said to a woman dressed in a white uniform at the top.

"Yes, Mr. Morris and companion, you will be at table four, which is on the port side by the third window. Enjoy your cruise."

"Cruise?" I asked as he led me to a quaint table for two on the left side of the boat. A single pink rose sat in a crystal vase, illuminated by a single candle.

"I wanted a special dinner, and I thought it would be good to get you away from everything else that you are constantly being bombarded with. There is nothing out here for the next three hours but you and I. So, here we are."

I estimated that there were twenty couples on board tonight, all seated at tables like ours. A steward took our coats and we were seated. A few minutes later a bell clanged a few times, and I could feel the roll of motion as the boat got underway.

Ian picked up a bottle from the pail next to the table, "Shall I?"

"Um, Ian, we're under age."

He laughed. "This is sparkling grape juice. They made a special accommodation for us." His eyes danced in the candlelight. And for the first time in my life, I was romanced.

CHAPTER 10

PROMISES

Early rains that were now flooding the Hudson Valley had replaced February's usual snows. Personally, I'd have preferred the snow; it didn't make me remember how close we were getting to my March deadline. The past two weeks had been a whirlwind of activities. For me personally, it had been spent meeting with Mrs. Vallente, trying to figure out how we were going to build the membership in our new support group, working with Chris trying to help him come to grips with what he was dealing with as he prepared to transition from male to female, trying to deal with how I felt about all of this as well as working on deciphering the clue that I had to solve in order to break the curse.

This on its own would have been bad enough, but I was now in the midst of also trying to figure out which college I would be attending and trying to keep my grades high enough so that I would still graduate with honors. If I lived that long.

Things were getting a bit complicated. What I wanted to be doing right now was taking a few hours to work on my little Sonex, but the reality was that I needed to get through the curse, or the Sonex would be worthless to me.

Currently, I was riding with Ian back to New Paltz to once again go to the university library there. We had tried several variations of ideas to solve the clues that I had been given, but we still hadn't quite found the right combination.

"How are you doing, Stevie?"

"About as well as I can," I answered with slight shrug.

"I thought I should let you know, I talked to Chris last night. He looked a bit different. It took me a while to notice that his eyebrows were thinned and more arched. He almost looked like a girl. When I mentioned it, he got all flustered for a minute, and then asked if we could speak in private."

I looked over, concerned since as far as I knew, I was the only one outside of Chris' family that knew that he was transgendered. "Is he okay?" I asked trying to sound nonchalant.

Ian looked over at me. "Stevie, Chris told me about Chrissy. He said you knew, and that we could talk about it."

Okay, now I was stuck. I was guarding a secret, that my boyfriend had maybe guessed, and now he wanted to talk to me about it. Either way, I was going to be walking a very narrow line. "Ian, I'm not sure what to say. I was told things in confidence, and I don't want to break that if…"

"Stevie, I know. You found out about Chrissy while you were at the little cabin behind the marina just before Valentines."

"Um," now what did I do? "Let me text Chris, okay?" I hated this; not trusting the man I loved about another friend's secret.

Ian just nodded as we made our way towards the library. My phone sounded with an incoming text, it was Chris letting me know I could talk. I let out a breath that I was unaware of holding. "I'm sorry, Ian, but I had to be sure."

He took my hand, kissed it and smiled at me, "That's why I love you, my responsible love."

For the rest of the ride, we discussed what our friend was facing.

Long sessions of delving through old text books about various cultures is not something that I enjoyed, but it was something that I had resigned myself to do. All I could use to push myself forward was the hopes that I would be alive after the equinox to enjoy the fruits of my labor. Too many of the books held opposing views on what various terms and symbols meant, which only meant that I was no closer to solving this clue than I was when started.

I slammed the current book closed and pulled out my phone, tapping the calendar feature. According to this, there was just shy of three weeks left to complete everything. I let my head fall to the table, where it hit the hard wood surface with an audible thud.

"Stevie," Ian called softly while shaking my shoulder. "I know that we've been at this for nearly three hours, but we've made some headway."

"Some headway?" I asked sarcastically. "We've got squat right now, Ian. I'm doomed."

"Hey! I don't want to hear any of that. We've found several resources that haven't told us what the symbols mean, but we have eliminated some. And," now he looked directly at me, "I think I've got a lead on some of the symbols. Well, at least the dog."

My head snapped in his direction. "What does it mean?"

"I'm not one hundred percent sure, but the use of a dog, specifically a hound, was used in medieval times on coats of arms for various families. We might be able to trace it back to some point of origin. Perhaps it was for one of your family members."

I thought about it for a moment, "I doubt it was for one of my ancestors. It would be more likely to be from Ichabod Crane's family. I mean the curse was placed on my family because of what they did to Crane. The witch is trying to teach me a lesson, so why would she give me something that would be a token from my ancestors?"

"Hmmm, that does make sense. Either way, it's a place to start."

"Guess that's something at least."

We stayed at the library for another half an hour before we decided to make our way back home. There was a question that was bugging me, but I ended up waiting until we were almost halfway home before I brought it up.

"Ian, I told you that Lerch wants me to talk to the student body about the new group, right?"

"Yeah. That should be exciting."

"Right," I sneered. "I've got to be honest; I'm scared to death about this. I'm not a public speaker, and just the thought of facing down the entire student body is really freaking me out."

"Mrs. Vallente is helping you, so that should make things a little better."

"We've got the basics covered. Mrs. Lerch is going to start the whole assembly, briefly talking about what happened with Damian. Then I'm supposed to get up and give reasons why they should join us. Mrs. Vallente is going to finish things off. I'm glad that they are going to be there to help, but it still scares me. Do you think many people will be willing to join?"

Ian hesitated, and I looked at him sharply. "What?" I asked.

"I don't know what to say. I think you're going to find that kids will talk a big game, but when they are asked to step forward and actually be counted, they behave like sheep; they're going to wait for someone else to take the first step."

Ian smiled at me, but it did little to relieve the fears that were now brewing in my mind. I'd hoped, perhaps optimistically, that the vast majority of the kids at school would be more than happy to jump into this new group. I'd known them for over a decade. Of course, they'd known Damian for about the same length of time, and look what they did there. I definitely was not happy about my current prospects.

Ian must have been able to sense this. "Stevie, listen, let's not worry about this right this moment. When the time comes, you'll find the right words to say that will make the difference. Right now what you need to concern yourself about is this clue."

I snorted, "Yeah, and I'm doing oh-so-well on that end aren't I?"

He took my hand, pulled it to his lips and kissed it tenderly. "You are quite possibly the bravest, strongest person that I know. You're smart and dependable. You've got friends and family that are here to help and support you through all of this. With a team like that, I know that you will make it through."

I leaned my head back, and the tears came unabashed. "Thanks. I love you, Ian."

"Love you too." He kissed my hand again, and I closed my eyes and dozed for the remainder of the ride.

"According to this," Ian said as he lifted the tattered leather bound book slightly. "The symbol of a dog was used during the medieval times to represent nobility. It would represent their loyalty and devotion to each other."

Emily, Chris, Ian and I were sitting in my living room, gathered around the fireplace. A collection of books was strewn across the coffee table and any other flat surface that we could commandeer. Mom was in the kitchen preparing a feast seeing that she wanted to have another group meeting.

"Well," Mom's voice rang out of the kitchen just before she appeared in the doorway. "In a strange way, that all makes sense."

I looked at her with a blank face, "Excuse me?"

She wiped her hands on the dishcloth that she had tucked into her waistband. "What I mean is that the medallion that you found had a picture of a dog, carrying a flower. According to what you've already found out, this whole curse thing started because an ancestor was indifferent to others. They put their ideas above everyone else. Perhaps Abraham Von Brunt descended from aristocracy."

Standing, I walked across the room to where a printed copy of the medallion lay on an end table. Staring at the picture, I focused on the symbols. "I don't think that Von Brunt was an aristocrat." I turned back and faced the room, "It seems to me, that he was the descendent of a shop owner or something. He was a normal person, who went to extraordinary lengths to get what he wanted, and didn't care if he stepped on someone else in the process."

"Sounds like several people we all know," Chris chimed in.

"I think that the nobility part of all this, if that is what it is, is from the witch's family tree," I stated flatly. My mind was again going in multiple directions, so I was lagging behind it.

"I'm not sure about that, Stevie," Ian declared. "If you remember, both you and Emily had dreams one night in which you were both subjected to paranormal experiences."

Shrugging my shoulders, I slumped back to the love seat and collapsed next to Ian. I kept running through it in my mind. "It seems that perhaps we are on to something here, but it just doesn't make sense."

"This is just starting to 'not make sense'?" Emily asked disbelieving. "This whole mess seems to be well above the normal content for any day."

"That's true," I agreed. "But what I was referring to is the idea that if the medallion was from the witch, then why is she trying to stop us? Why did she pull us into those dreams? Where is the relation that we need to see? It's almost as if there was another force that is working here as well."

"Yeah, that's just what we need," Chris whined. "Two of you have already had close encounters of the weird kind, multiple times for that matter. We're doing all of this on the belief that there actually is a curse that has been haunting your family for the past two-plus centuries. The whole idea is a little far-fetched if you ask me."

Once everyone else had arrived, we took a break from working on the clue, and tried to settle into a nice, relaxing family meal. Yeah, like that was going to happen right now. With nine of us crowding the table, everyone was talking over each other to the point that you could barely hear what anyone else was saying. Actually, this worked in my favor, since my mind was continuing to deliberate over what had been said earlier.

I had been so sure that there had to be some type of connection that would bring the medallion and the clue together,

I had ignored anything else. But could there be? What if some unknown spirit, witch or otherwise, was trying to throw me off track? How would I know?

Without realizing that I had let my mind wander so far, I had apparently frozen at the table. My fork raised part way up, my mouth open and my eyes staring blankly at the wall.

"Stevie?" I suddenly heard my dad's voice and felt a tap on my shoulder. "Stevie, you okay?"

"I'm sorry, what?" I realized that there was no other sound from anyone at the table.

"You just went blank and still," Mom said, with her voice quivering. "Did you have a vision?"

"No. I guess I just had a thought." I dropped my fork back to my plate, took a sip of my soda and told them about my most recent thoughts.

Sharing my innermost dreams was something that I had been doing with my family for years. Sharing secrets with Em and Chris was the same. Sharing both of these with Ian was a benefit that I was still getting used to, but the idea of sharing my insecurities with everyone was new to me. When I needed to talk to someone about my fears, often it was Mom, but tonight I was sitting here discussing them with eight other people.

"Looking at the big picture makes me wonder if I am on the right track or if I'm being led astray," I stated in the most confident voice I could manage.

Dad picked up his coffee cup and held it as if it were some kind of security blanket. "I can see where you might think that, Stevie. But here is another thought. Is it possible that we are looking at two sides of the same coin? What I mean is, if we accept that this curse was placed upon our family by a single witch, would it not be possible that she had other relatives?

"That's an interesting point, Mr. Nixon," Ian said thoughtfully. "My Aunt practices 'white magic' as you would call it. I know that she says that whatever you send out will come back on you, in a greater degree. If this witch sent this curse out, did the rebound fall on her own family."

"What would that do?" Emily wanted to know.

Ian looked around and then continued with his thought. "What if when this curse was cast, not only did it affect Stevie's family, but also the caster's family? It's possible that the witch's family is trapped between plains of existence or something. They need the curse broken in order to pass on."

"But then why would one of them try to stop it?" I demanded.

Nonni spoke up for the first time, "Maybe the whole dilemma caused a family rift?"

"What?" I asked, totally lost.

"I just wonder what the result of the curse was on the family. If the first witch was so upset that she would cast this type of a spell, maybe she intentionally damned herself. But when the curse came back on her own family, they're now trapped. One side wants you to fail; seeks your death and another soul in payback for what was done to her kin. The other wants you to win so that they may finally find peace."

Realizing what implications this would have, wondering how many souls were now in the balance of my actions, only amplified the urgency that I felt. I'd never wanted to be the poster person for anything; I kind of liked hiding in the back and doing the unseen work. Now I was being pushed to the forefront in several areas; the group at school and the potential freedom of who knew how many souls. This was more pressure than I could handle.

I quickly excused myself from the table, and took a moment to make a break for it and sneaked out the back door. Misty was the only one who followed me. I looked up at the starry sky and imagined things like they use to be before all of this began.

Misty jumped so that her front paws were just above my knees, and pressed her head into my leg. Absently, I reached down and scratched her. "I know, girl. I just wish I knew what to do."

CHAPTER 11

DISTANCE

March pounded into Sleepy Hollow like a lion with a vengeance. I sat in my room watching the rain streak down the window as lightening flashed across the sky. I'd always loved a good thunderstorm, but I was finding that it wasn't the most productive scenario when it came to getting homework done. My concentration kept going to the storm outside the window instead of working through the integration problems I was trying to solve for Calculus.

Looking back at my notes, I again tried to understand what Mr. Sweeny had been referring to when he taught us about integration by parts and then called it the "voodoo" integration. Whatever he had meant during class today was now escaping me, and I still had another twenty problems to work through.

I kept plugging away for another fifteen minutes before I gave up and sent a text to Ian, hoping that he was having more luck with this than I was. Setting the phone down on my desk so that I wouldn't keep staring at it waiting for his response, I looked back towards the window.

Misty jumped up onto my lap, and I absently began scratching her ears while my mind wandered the current situation.

Over the past few weeks, Chris had told Emily and Ian about what was going on with him, and we were all trying to stay supportive. Mark had given him a slight reprieve, only because the psychiatrist had demanded it. There were still tensions in his home life, but the end of the school year was coming up fast, which would allow Chris to move forward with his transition. Hopefully, that would resolve many of the issues that they were facing.

On my own front, I still felt like I was falling behind on my quest. I had a little over two weeks left to figure things out, but here I sat moaning over the "voodoo" stuff.

Feeling sorry for myself, I grabbed my cup of tea and padded over to the window seat and curled my feet underneath to watch the show. Sensing an opportunity, Misty leapt onto my lap, wiggling her way up until she was able to curl into my shoulder. So, there I sat, cradling her like a baby, watching the storm blow through and telling myself that I had every right to be afraid of what was going on. Regardless of how logical I told myself this was, I knew that they were only excuses for my failing to see what I was sure was right before my eyes.

Searching in my mind, I brought up the memory of the night that I dreamt about going to the clearing and facing the witch. The more that I thought about things, the more that I felt everyone else was right; there was more than one witch involved here. I had no idea how to deal with a single witch, let alone a coven.

I knew instinctively, that I would have to make some hard decisions soon. I couldn't keep splitting my time worrying about the kids at school and trying to figure out the clue. It would end up being one or the other. Resolved, I sipped my tea, and tried to think about what I was going to say tomorrow to Mrs. Vallente.

Dreams that night were frightening. I found myself alternately burning at a stake, the fire so real, I could feel it scorching my legs and hands. Then I was being chased through the forest by a horseman, who had a pumpkin where his head was supposed to have been. I was thrashing around so much that I ended up getting my feet wrapped together in the blankets and fell out of bed.

Opening my eyes in the darkened room, with the sound of howling wind outside was more terrifying than any thing that I had experienced yet. As I lay on the floor, trying to get my bearings, I took stock of my condition.

Again, my clothes were wet, as if I had been in that forest in the pounding rain. My legs were sore; both in the feeling that the muscles had been abused from a hard run, but my skin hurt as well. Carefully, I unwrapped the blanket and gaped at what I saw. My skin was discolored and puffy. Scrambling back to the nightstand, I flipped on the light. My legs were covered by the red sores of first and second degree burns.

"This is getting way too personal!" I screamed into the empty night.

Remembering that it was very early morning, and that the rest of my family was hopefully sleeping, I kept the rest of my rant to mere mutters. Unfortunately, my mom has hearing that will pick up a child in distress from a quarter mile away.

The door creaked open, "Stevie," she said as she came in and saw me huddled on the floor with the blankets wrapped around my shoulders and tears streaming down my cheeks.

"Mom," I whimpered. "It hurts! Why is this happening to me? Why is she trying to kill me?"

"What happened, Honey?" she asked. Sitting on the edge of the bed, she pulled me up and cradled me in her arms. Soothing me with her touch and the soft ease of her voice.

I cried for minutes, soaking her robe, but she just sat and kept consoling me. Finally, I was able to look up and try to give her an answer. "I had another one of those realistic dreams." I told her what had happened, her eyes getting wide with concern as I told her about burning.

She peeled back the covers, and looked at my swollen legs. "Oh, God, Stevie! This is getting out of hand." She fought to reign in her emotions and keep a cool head and then turned to me, "Let's get these cleaned up and put some ointment on them. Hopefully it will turn out to be nothing too serious."

Forty minutes later, I was lying in my bed, Mom was lying next to me stroking my hair and trying to relax me enough to go back to sleep. It wasn't going to matter, either way I was going to have deep dark shadows under my eyes for the next few days.

School the next day was dreadful. Not only did I have to deal with the fact that my face had dark circles around the eyes large enough that I could be mistaken for a raccoon, but for some reason the moment that I stepped foot on the campus, Tanya and Gabby decided that it was open season. It started with nothing more than me trying to walk into the building, and getting sprayed with silly string. On its own, this wouldn't be horrible, but when they figured that they weren't going to get a rise out of me, they resorted to throwing the cans at me. Why? I've got no idea.

When I turned to face them, they claimed that I had provoked them, so now I was cooling my heels waiting at the principal's office for the second time in my career. When Mrs. Lerch saw me, she chuckled and waved me into her office. Fifteen minutes later, she was still laughing, and I was on my way to clean up.

Grabbing my coat out of my locker, I headed for the door. Before this whole curse mess, I would have never thought about skipping out of school. Over the past few months, it had happened twice. Escaping from the clutches of the educational system for the day, I headed over to Scoops.

Ignoring the bell that rang when the door was opened and the little sign that said they would like to seat you, I made my way to the corner booth. Nodding to the waitress Terri, I pushed into the corner as far as I could. I needed the solitude and time to pull myself together.

I sat there sipping a cup of cocoa, and savoring a fudge brownie and contemplated what my next series of moves should be. On a paper I had listed what I considered to be the facts of the situation. All I really knew for certain was that I had now had two episodes where it appeared that I had been taken into an alternate world that was occupied by witches and who knows what else.

With that came the realization: Ian was right, not all of them wanted me to survive this.

Thinking that I was nearing the point of really needing a counselor, I tried to ignore all of the distractions that came from the patrons around me. The scraping of chairs on the worn tile, the jingle of the bell as the door opened and closed, the muted conversations that they were having with each other. I didn't even notice the shadow that fell across the table as I contemplatively stared into the empty cup of hot chocolate.

When the chair next to me was roughly dragged out, I jumped and looked at the figure next to me who was now silhouetted by the large window.

"Stevie," Ian's voice broke into my solitude. "You okay? You gave a few of us a bit of a shock running out like that."

I could feel the tears welling in the corner of my eyes and knew that if I tried to speak right now, I would only break down and cry. In way of an answer, I just shook my head.

Ian sat and then pulled me into him so that I could cry on his shoulder. His left hand pulled my waist while his right hand slowly rubbed my back. He only stopped for a moment when the bell over the door rang again and he motioned to someone.

Working to overcome the desire to just stay burrowed in Ian's grasp, I slowly turned my head and opened my eyes. I could make out Emily and Chris moving through the collection of tables making their way to where we were. When I had bolted out of the school an hour ago, it was to give me time to be away from it all. Now I had all of my friends, skipping class for me, just to be sure that I was safe.

"What are you guys doing here?" I asked looking at Emily.

"Ian saw you making a break for it," she answered. "We figured this was where you'd run to, so we had a quick meeting and figured out when we could each sneak out and get here to help."

"And what would you have done if I wasn't here?"

Chris laughed, "Stevie, you're kind of predictable. When you get upset, you want a corner, hot chocolate and you want it ASAP. This was the only place that fit the bill."

Emily continued, "Besides, Ian was heading out first. The plan was simple; he would text us when he got here. We know all of your hiding spots."

Help from my friends was enough to calm me down and convince me that returning to school was going to be the best move. The four of us stood and walked slowly out and across the street to the school. Seeing the lone figure waiting at the doors, I knew that I was busted again, but I was determined that I would not let my friends get punished for helping me survive.

Unfortunately, Mrs. Lerch didn't see things my way. She felt that it was irresponsible for me to have rushed out of the building like I did, which earned me a day of In School Suspension. I was sure that this was going to go over really well with my folks.

By the time that I got to lunch, I was beyond furious about the whole episode. Not only did I have ISS, but also she had given Ian, Chris and Emily two nights of detention!

To make things even worse, I found out that neither Gabby nor Tanya, who were the ones who had instigated the whole thing, had any kind of punishment at all. I just crossed my arms on the table and laid my head on them.

Listening to my classmates joking around did little to ease my frustration during the next few classes. I was sure that I was living in a soon-to-be-declared disaster area, and it was only a matter of time before the whole place crashed in around my head.

When the final bell sounded, I quickly got my things from my locker and headed out to catch a bus home. It was lonely heading home with out Chris or Emily, but since my mom had texted me and left little in the way of wiggle room in the order of come right home, I figured the best that I could do was comply. I mean, I was doomed any way, but perhaps I could convince my parents to cancel my grounding after graduation.

"Stevie," Mom said as soon as I walked in the door. She used a tone of voice that we didn't hear often; it was the one where you felt your entire spinal cord freeze the moment you heard it. She appeared in the door, her hands wringing a dishcloth, "I'm waiting for your brilliant reason for skipping classes today, and to find out how you intend to tell your father about your day of ISS tomorrow."

My head fell. "Mom, I'm sorry. It's just that, um, Gab, things happened and I lost control."

"You lost control?" she snapped, her temper was flaring making this place that I really didn't want to be. "You lost control, again! We've talked about this many times. I know that right now you are dealing with a huge amount of stress. To be honest, I can't imagine everything, but you have a little problem at school, with a girl who had given you issues for ten years, and that you can't pull off." She dropped into a chair, "Can you try to explain it to me?"

Flopping onto the couch, I exhaled in one huge huff. "I'm not sleeping at night, you know that, you've been in during the nightmares. Well, I'm still having them, and last night was a doozey. So, I go do the responsible thing today and go to school with bags under my eyes that are big enough to pack for a two-week cruise, and the first people I see are Gabby and Tanya. Their normal pleasantries aren't enough, so when I turn my back on them they start throwing things at me. And what happens? I'm the one who get in trouble." I jumped up and began pacing the room.

"I'm the one who has to shoulder this whole blasted mess, and no one seems to care!" I screamed before I raced for the stairs.

Realizing that my emotions were all over the board right now, I know that the smartest thing that I could do was to find a quiet place to try and settle down so I didn't begin hurling everything I could put my hands on. Racing into my room, I slammed the door shut and flopped onto the window seat and leaned my head back. My fists were clenched in rage, and my entire body shook.

"Bloody witches and their stupid curses. I wish Icabod had killed good old Abraham Von Brunt. Then this stupid curse wouldn't be here and I could maybe have a normal life," I snarled under my breath.

My fists were still flexing, trying to work the anger out when I heard the door to my room creak open.

My eyes flashed open filled with fury. Without thinking, I grabbed something off of my desk and heaved it towards the door, where it disintegrated in a loud crash. At the soft yip, my head turned towards the sound.

Misty lay amongst the shards of what had been a jewelry box, now scattered about on the floor, near the door. She was whimpering and shaking, blood trickled from her leg.

"Oh, Misty," the sound caught in my throat. "I'm sorry girl." As I neared her, her shaking increased, and she hopped up on her three uninjured legs. Her little stub of a tail was now tucked as far under her body as she could get it. Her head was low, eyes wide in fear and she backed away from me.

With every step I took nearer, she hobbled back three, whimpering with each step and leaving a trail of blood on the floor.

"Mom!" I yelled, tears were now thick in my voice and flooding my eyes. "Mom, Please come quick! Misty is hurt."

"What happened?" she called as she came up the stairs. "I heard the crash, but how did she get hurt?" Clearing the top stair, she saw the pup, now cowering in the corner, still shaking.

"Mom, I threw something when I heard my door open. I wanted to be alone, and I overreacted. I think she got hit with some of the fallout. But she won't even come near me."

"Stevie, go back into your room and clean up the mess. I'll take care of Misty."

I stepped slowly back to my room, and leaned on the doorframe. Mom scooped up the terrified dog, and cuddled her as she walked down the stairs.

Watching the whole scene had devastated me. I closed the door, swept up the shards of porcelain and flopped onto the bed. I knew that I was responsible for so much of what was happening right now, and I didn't like it. The weight of the curse was taking its toll on me; I realized that if I just stopped trying, it would all be over very soon.

I didn't want to think about how people would feel when I was gone, but if I just let go, it would definitely be easier on me. There would be no one to injure Misty with flying jewelry boxes, no one to cause my friends to do stupid things like skip class. If I were gone, my parents wouldn't have to worry so much anymore.

Somewhere in the midst of these thoughts, I decided to just let go. Crying myself to sleep, I let the dreams wash over me.

Darkness loomed over the land, broken only by the fire in the clearing. I recognized this place, as it was the one that I had been to the last time, when I burned.

"Ye've come to me in the dark of night. Hast thou decided to do what's right?" the witch asked.

I was about to agree, when white smoke appeared in the clearing, and coalesced into a young woman with raven black hair in a silver gown. "Daughter," she said looking at me, "you must not give up the fight, on this or any other night. The anger from the wicked now burns bright, but you must choose the path that's right. You are not alone on this task. We are here to help if you but ask. You are smart and you must be clever, for if you give up we're all damned forever."

Stunned, I mumbled, "Help me please."

CHAPTER 12

DISCOVERIES

Four days had passed since the whole incident at home. Misty still wouldn't come to me, and if I walked into a room where she was, she immediately tucked her tail and would slink out. It was breaking my heart.

I couldn't really dwell on it. In my dream, I'd asked for help and in a flash I had been transported back to my own bed. The help that I had received was more in the form of my friends finding bits and pieces that when we put together had led us to a few new ideas. I figured that the good witch, as I had taken to thinking of her, had done her part by letting me get a few good nights sleep. Now I needed to do mine.

After waking the next morning, I had focused myself on finding the answer to the clue that would bring peace to my family. Thus far it had totally eluded me, though. Today we were heading to the library to check on some old texts that Emily had happened to find in an on-line search.

Everyone else was hopeful that somewhere in the piles of dusty books, the answer that I was looking for was hidden.

Reaching into my bag, I pulled out my phone to check the name of whom I was to see for the books. My eyes noticed the date; I had less than two weeks now and it was going fast.

Inside the library, I walked over to the reference desk. "May I help you?" a short gray haired librarian asked.

""Um, hi. My name is Stevie Nixon, and a friend mentioned that I should speak to a Ms. Helen Urbanski. Is she available?"

The woman smiled, and removed her plastic framed tri-focals, "Well since I'd be Helen Urbanski, I guess I'm available."

Over the next ten minutes, I gave Helen a quick run down of what it was that I was trying to locate. She led me down into the basement and to a door. I had seen this door every time that I had come down here, but since it is marked for employees only, I never tried to find out what was on the other side. Helen pushed the door open, and ushered me in.

When the lights flickered on, I was surprised to find myself standing in what could have passed for a high tech lab. Machines hummed and I could feel a cool movement of air across my face.

"This is the rare book collection. You can only be here with one of the librarians, and the books may not leave this room." She walked down the narrow path between specialized display cases that were lined with books. "The images that you showed me look to be something that would have been in vogue somewhere during the late eighteenth century. So, we'll try here first."

She stopped at a large case, where several leather bound tomes were isolated. Donning cotton gloves, she carefully reached through the special openings on the side of the box and moved a book to the rack directly under the glass top. Paging through the book, she found images that bore a close resemblance to the images that I had found on the medal and on the actual clue.

"I think this may be as close as we can get here, Stevie. Would you like a copy of this section of the book?"

"Yes. Please," I answered excitedly.

Helen used a special digital camera and took several pictures of the pages that we were interested in, pressed a button and finally replaced the book back in its spot. Removing her gloves, she led me back towards the door. Just inside, she stooped over to pick up a pack of pages that had been printed out. "Here you go, dear. Hope this helps with your research project."

"Thanks." As we left the rare book collection, I tried to walk and skim the pages that I'd just picked up. My luck was running par for the course. I walked right into another patron and ended up wearing his cappuccino.

Even having a coffee stained blouse wasn't going to bring down my mood right now.

Finding a table near the back entrance, I sat waiting for Ian, Emily and Chris. Flipping through the pages from Helen, I tried to notice the variations of each of the symbols. It seemed to me that many of them looked very similar, but were used to mean different things.

"Daydreaming again?" Ian asked as he tugged on my sleeve and pulled me up for a quick kiss.

"No. And hi," I responded with a kiss of my own. "I met with the librarian in the reference section, and she was able to give us an approximation of when the symbols would have been used. From that, she was able to make prints of these," I said gesturing at the pile of papers that were on the table.

Emily picked the pages up and scanned them quickly herself while Chris looked over her shoulder. I took a double take of Chris. It seemed that now that we knew about Chrissy, the lines were beginning to blur. I have to admit, the light pink lipstick was cute.

We delved into the pile of papers and then basing off of the conversation that Helen and I had while we were in the rare books, we began to scour the library for books that talked about the use of symbols during the time period. Within two hours, our table was scattered with nearly thirty books, what looked to be a full ream of print outs and our assortments of notebooks.

Ian kept going back to a book that concentrated on the use of witchcraft during the late eighteenth century. "I feel like there is something in here that I need to be aware of," he said when he caught me looking at him.

I shrugged. "I didn't say anything. But out of curiosity, is the feeling for solving the clue or is it something else?"

He laid the book on the table. "Stevie, I haven't stopped thinking about the clue. I wish I knew what to say about the feeling though. It is almost a compulsion that is driving me into this part of history. Like there is a link that I'm missing, and once I've got it, it will help you with your quest."

I reached over, and took his hand. He blushed ever so slightly. I was still amazed that I could even have this kind of an effect on someone. "You'll figure it out. I have faith in you," with a sigh and an eye roll, "it's me that I don't have faith in,"

"Hey, Girl," Emily casually remarked. "You know that you've got all of us as a support team here. We're going to get you through all of this. Relax."

"Easier said than done, Em. But, thanks you guys for all of the help and the support."

Chris smiled and draped an arm over my shoulder. "That's what friends are for."

Watching everyone work on my behalf for two and a half hours was a lifting experience. I knew that my friends were doing everything that they could to not let me down. I was just hoping that my efforts wouldn't let them down either. The unfortunate part was, that now after we had spent those two and a half hours, we didn't seem to have made much progress. I was feeling that I was losing my drive to continue.

Apparently somewhere in this time frame, Ian found something that jogged his memory. "I think I know what I've been missing," he announced.

"Huh?" was my brilliant response.

"Back to day dreaming? I think I've seen some of the related materials that were listed in this book at my Grandmother's house. I think I'm going to take a run over there and paw through them. Maybe I'll even give my mom a call, and she can give me a hand with things."

"Uh, yeah, sure." I was getting the message that it was going to take more than one or two brain cells working to get a coherent thought out of me. I blinked twice as Ian pulled on his coat. "See ya then."

Emily leaned across the table and poked me. "You okay, Stevie? You seem to be out in your own little world there."

I smiled and tried to give her a glib response, "It's okay though, they know me here."

She laughed and shook her head before she went back into her book.

I'm not sure what happened next. I remember sitting at the table and Emily squealed with excitement. She was shoving a book under my nose pointing at something. Chris leaned over and read something from his book that seemed to perhaps correlate with it. But I was in a fog.

The mist slowly curled up from the warm ground in the cool night. The fire burned bright in the clearing, and the witch was there. Tonight she was dressed in black flowing robes and there was a gleam in her eye.

"Less than a fortnight is all ye have. Surrender now; ye cannot be saved; know the power of the clan of Crane. Your life is now and forever ruined." Her arm reached out for me.

I screamed, and turned to run. Running aimlessly through the brush rushing to be far away from her. I heard the pounding of hooves. Were they chasing or helping? There was no time to wonder right now. I had to find a way back to reality; to Ian, Emily, Chris and my family. I needed to go back before she did real harm to me.

A horse crashed through the undergrowth and I stared at its rider. He was a tall man, with big broad shoulders. He was dressed in the clothes of a military man. Where his head should have been, there was a jack-o-lantern. I was now face-to-face with my how-ever-many-greats grandfather: Abraham Von Brunt, the Headless Horseman.

Confused, I just stood there unable to move. My brain was working overtime trying to fuse reality and my dream together.

The horseman stared at me for a moment. "Be strong kinswoman." He nudge the horse, and they disappeared into the forest again.

Voices broke through the forest night again. But these voices were familiar. "Chris, you'd better call her mom. Come on, Stevie, snap out of it."

I focused on Emily's voice. The cool mist began to dissipate, and I felt hands on my arms. Opening my eyes, I slowly realized that I was no longer sitting at the table. I was now flat on my back in the center of a throng of people surrounding me. "What happened?" I whispered.

"Hah! You're back! Chris, let Mrs. Nixon know that she woke up." Emily gently caressed my head. "You gave us all a scare there, kiddo. One minute you were looking through a book, and the next minute, you're on the floor screaming and looking like you're trying to run from something."

I tried to move, but the blinding headache raced through and left me feeling nauseous. "Excuse us please," a voice commanded from the back of the crowd. Two paramedics came in wheeling a gurney.

I groaned. How embarrassing. Could it get any worse? "Stevie!" I heard my mom's voice shriek as I caught a glimpse of her and Dad running in.

Despite my protests, I was loaded up on the gurney, patrons of the library stood silently as I was paraded towards the exit and the waiting ambulance. To make matters worse, Ian ran up just as they were loading me in.

Doctors were waiting in the hallway for us when we pulled into the hospital. Immediately, they seemed to pounce on me checking the various vitals. I was wheeled into a room and a nurse in efficient green scrubs pulled the curtain around me. "Can you give me your name?"

"I'm Stevie Nixon."

"Okay, Stevie, we've got to run several tests to determine your overall health. We'll begin those tests in a few minutes. Can you remember anything before you collapsed?"

"I was at the library researching," I paused to edit myself. I didn't want anyone here to find out about my fighting against witches and the headless Horseman. All that would do was get me a one-way ticket to the Looney Bin. "I was researching the symbols on my family crest. It's a project for school. I was with Chris and Emily."

"Okay, so your memory seems to be fine about events prior to the seizure."

"Seizure? I didn't have a seizure." I couldn't have a seizure. That would affect my flying. No seizures. Period.

"It's okay, Stevie. We'll know everything after we finish our testing.

For the next three hours, I endured every test that they could think up. I had a C.T. scan, an M.R.I. and two rounds of x-rays. In the end, they pronounced me healthy, and they had no explanation of what had caused the episode. From hearing the doctor talk to my parents, they were writing it off as possibly low blood sugar. *Sure*, I thought, *let's go with that.*

Afraid to close my eyes, I sat in the back seat of the car watching the world go by. My mind was trying to absorb everything that had happened over the past few hours. The problem was, that if I tried to think about the reality of the situation, I began shaking uncontrollably. Mom kept thinking that this was another round of unexplained seizures and thought maybe we should return to the doctors.

The only option that seemed viable was to tell them what happened. So, as we drove around the state park on the way home, I told them about the witch and the Horseman. By the time we pulled into the house, we were all shaking a bit.

Kyle came out on the porch flanked by Ian and Emily with Chris in the back. Before I could try to stand, I felt myself being lifted out of the car and Ian carried me inside. "I'm not an invalid," I protested.

Ian leaned over, "Stevie, I've never been that scared before. Now stop squirming, or I'm likely to drop you."

Laughing, I relaxed.

As soon as we had made it into the house, Ian deposited me on the couch in the family room. Mom had a thick quilt that she wrapped me in and Dad was starting a fire. My friends all sat in chairs around me and there was talk of hot cocoa. My world seemed to be all right.

Then I saw Misty. She looked at me with those spaniel eyes, but when I motioned and called her, she slunk back out to the kitchen.

"Does something hurt?" Emily asked, noting the tear dripping down my cheek.

I shook my head. "I think I've just been under too much stress these last few weeks, and with everything coming to a head right now, it just overwhelmed me."

"You know what you need? You need to have a day of pampering out with the girls."

I glared at Emily. I had issues of being in a spa. Perhaps it stemmed from the incident when I was five. I'd gone with my mom to her spa, and while she was in the chair I was playing on the floor near her. Not being aware enough, I ended up getting into some of the chemicals that were stored under the sink. It took three years before my hair was anywhere close to being its natural color.

Emily knew this. But she glared back at me with that pink streak of stubbornness. "It'll be fun!"

"Noooo!" I yelled as she walked away.

CHAPTER 13

WASHOUT

Saturday morning was cool and clear. I'd let myself sleep in for a little bit, hoping to recharge my batteries. I'm not sure if it had really worked or not, but for the first time in several weeks, I didn't wake up thinking about taking an afternoon nap.

I spent a little time in my room, poking through the various notes that I had assimilated on the clue. I still wasn't sure what the hieroglyphics meant, but I felt that now that we had at least taken the first step towards breaking the clue, we were making progress. I knew from physics that once you got some momentum, it was hard to stop.

Voices carried to my window, and I looked out to see Kyle playing with an excited Misty. I watched for more than a few minutes, wishing that I could take back my tantrum that had caused her to be wary of me. I'd give almost anything to be able to get back on an even keel with my own dog.

I knew that my life was in serious trouble.

Within an hour, my frustration level had risen to the point that I was no longer able to clearly think about what I was trying to do. Sighing, I shoved all of the materials back into my backpack, and figured that I'd head down to the library after breakfast and spend the day just sorting through some of the old books to see if the mysterious term every showed up.

Opening my door, I started down the hall and saw Misty at the top of the stairs. Kneeling down, I called her, "Hey there, little girl, come on."

She just looked at me, tucked her tail and scooted back down. I watched her go, "I promise you, Misty, someday, I'll earn your trust again."

"You promising her, or yourself?" Kyle asked from his doorway.

Closing my eyes to help hold my embarrassment, I stood up. "I guess both. I miss having her close by. I was stupid, for only a minute, but I'm paying a very steep price for it."

He gave me a quick hug before he returned to the depths of his room to do what ever he was planning for a spring morning.

Mom was in the kitchen making pancakes when I walked in. "Good morning!" she said in that exaggerated way parents do. "What's on your agenda for today?"

"I figured that I'd grab breakfast and then head down to the library. I'm hitting a wall with the clue. We've made some progress, but it's not solved yet. Do you think Dad would be able to give me a lift?"

She paused and thought for a moment. "Yeah, he probably should be able to. He was going to go to the airport today to help your grandfather with something over there. I think that he was going to see if you'd like to go along."

"Oh. I'd like to see Nonni and Poppy, but this who curse thing has me going nuts."

"You go to the library, and we'll make a point of going to see everyone later this week, okay?" The ring of the phone interrupted her. "Hello?" she answered. "Just a minute, Emily." Mom held the phone out to me.

"Hey, Em. What's up?"

"Get your purse, I'll be there in five minutes. I've got a surprise for you."

"Em, I've got things to do today."

"Stevie, when I asked what you were doing today, you gave me the runaround about working on that clue. Now, I know that it is all-important and stuff, but you need a break to reduce your stress level, girl. I'll see you in five."

The phone went dead and I just stared at the hand piece. "What was that about?" Mom asked.

"I'm getting the feeling that I'm about to be abducted. Em is coming to pick me up for a surprise."

"That should be fun."

"Personally, with everything else that is going on, I think I'd rather go to the library." I grabbed my purse as I heard the sound of a car pulling into my driveway. I decided to really grasp for a way to get out of this. "Any chance you could tell her that I'm grounded? Or, maybe I need to help you alphabetize the m&m's for an upcoming party or something."

Mom smiled. "No! Perhaps it would be good for you to get out of here for a while. Besides, I'm not going to condone lying to someone." She stepped by me to get the knock on the door.

Pulling the door open, Mom stepped to the side to let people in. From my seat in the kitchen, I heard what had to be at least three other voices. Wonderful, I thought. At least all of the voices seemed to be in high spirits. I shoved off of the stool and headed towards the door.

Walking into the hall, I saw Emily's blue and pink hair bobbing around behind my mom. There were two other girls that

I knew a bit from school, but I didn't hang around with them often.

Delia O'Brien was about as tall as I was, with pale blue eyes and looked like she could play defensive line without much trouble. Beside her I saw the highlighted auburn hair that matched the perky voice of Nicole Lapp. Nicole was only about five feet tall, but she was had the body that made every guy in the school drool.

I had had classes with Nicole, and Dee was a recent transplant from Ireland who now lived next to Emily. But to say that either of them was a close personal friend would have been quite a stretch.

Sliding by the other girls in the hall, Emily came over. "Have we got plans for you," she said.

"Em, I'm kind of flattered that you want to get me out and away and all, but I'm running out of time. There are only a few days until we hit the equinox," I put my hand on her shoulder. "It's going to be curtains for me, you know what I mean?" I asked quietly.

"Stevie, you've been my best friend since forever. You've been working too hard on getting to the bottom of all of this. You need time to relax and recharge. That's why we've set things up for the four of us to hit Sylvia's for the works today."

I shot her a glare. "Em, Sylvia's is expensive. I'm not wasting my money on getting my nails done. I've been saving for a radio for the Sonex and working on it tends to kill my nails anyway. This is stupid."

"Hey, don't get your panties in a twist," she ordered. "You're not paying for it, I am. It's my treat, so just buck up and enjoy it. Let's go!" she said as she grabbed my arm and pulled me towards the door.

Someone tossed my coat over my head, blocking my view, as I was being pushed and pulled out of the door. I heard my mom yell out, "Have fun!" before the door slammed shut.

Great, I *am* being abducted. By teenage mutant aliens.

Going to a spa for the day could be a very relaxing thing, if it was what you wanted to be doing. Going against your will, as I was, left little room for me to recharge. This was a ridiculous waste of time. Well, they could force me to be there physically, but mentally, I would just keep working on the clue. I reached into my purse, and pulled out a small notebook and a pen. I closed my eyes and willed myself to bring the clue back into my mind.

The medallion had a dog, a flower and the hieroglyphics. The parchment had the same symbols. What was the relation between the dog the flower and the word?

I jumped when something sharp poked me in the side, "Ouch!"

"Hey we're going here to have fun," Dee said in her wonderful brogue. "Emily said no letting you work or think about your problems."

I opened one eye. "I'm not. I was trying to think about some ideas for a gift that I'm going to need for my…" I hesitated. I'd seen Emily's eyes focus on me in the rear view mirror so she was listening. She also knew everyone in my family, and with the way my luck was running knew their birthdays better than I did. "Okay, okay, I was thinking about a problem that I'm trying to solve for a friend." I put the notebook back into my purse. "I'll be good. No more thinking or worrying, I'll just concentrate on unlaxing and rewinding," I promised, intentionally mixing the words.

Sylvia's sits on the corner of Broadway and Dixon Street in Tarrytown. The décor of the place always struck me as being a bit on the obsessive side with almost the entire façade covered in ivy. Plants hung from hangers just outside the door, and inside as well. Gold lamé was draped over almost every surface.

"Oh, hello, hello! I'm Jenna, and I'll be working with," she paused and looked at the card in her hand, "ah yes, I'll be working with Stevie today."

I felt a slight shove in the back from Emily, which propelled me forward. "I'm Stevie," I said slightly waving my hand.

Jenna looked at me, her black eyes widened and her face seemed to pale as her lips went straight. "Okay then. It looks like we've got a bit of work to do," she said as she dragged me through a beaded curtain towards the unknown.

Okay, let me update my thoughts. I've been abducted by sadistic-teenage-mutant-aliens. I'd be lucky to survive *until* the equinox at this rate.

Sitting in the room that was obscured by the beaded curtain, was a small sink, a counter that seemed to be a cross between a porcupine and an electric appliance store and a barber chair. Jenna crossed to the chair, and grabbed a gown that had been carefully laid across the back of the chair and handed it to me.

"Go into the changing room over there and put this on," Jenna ordered.

I slowly shuffled into the room and put on the ridiculous gown. It left more of my leg exposed than any other piece of clothing I'd ever worn with the exception of a bathing suit. I looked around for a towel or something similar to wrap around my waist before I returned, but found nothing.

"C'mon, Stevie," Jenna said. "We've got a lot to do for you today, and there isn't much time to do it in."

For the next hour, Jenna washed, rinsed trimmed and attempted to style my hair. My hair has had many run-ins with would be stylists over the years, and is currently undefeated. This would be why I wear it long and in some kind of braid or ponytail. When it is left loose, or even worse styled, it takes on the appearance of the bride of Frankenstein. After she's been electrocuted.

Listening to Jenna's muttered curses, I could only guess that once again, my hair was on its way to dooming another stylist. I tried to take solace in that and closed my eyes.

"That's it!" Jenna exclaimed. "That mop that you call hair is too unruly! Since you won't let me cut it, I give up on it. C'mon now, let's get your facial started."

Jenna grabbed my hand and dragged me into another adjoining room and had me lay flat on my back. Without much fanfare, she began slinging mud onto my face and rubbing in into my cheeks. I had to admit, that the massaging motion did feel relaxing.

Apparently I'd dozed off while lying there. I became aware of several voices: Emily, Dee and Nicole were somewhere around.

"It looks like someone took a weed-wacker to her hair," Nicole whispered, stifling back a giggle.

"She looks like a fallen leprechaun. The tangled mass of hair, the muddy face and the grim look on her face," Dee added.

"Check out the picture! I wonder how we can get it as her picture on FaceBook?" Emily added with a laugh.

"I can hear you," I said.

"That you in there, Stevie? Or should I say Miss Messy?" Emily threw in trying to be funny. "Stevie, I've got to say, you look like a mess."

"It's your fault! I wanted to go to the library, but no! I've got to come here so that the stylist can insult me, and then my so-called friends can make fun of me."

"Hey, it's all in good fun," Emily laughed. An audible BING rang through the room. "Hey check out the comments that that picture just got. It's going viral!"

I sprang from the bed, dripping mud everywhere. "Tell me you did not just post a picture of me lying there with my hair in a rat's nest, covered in this goo wearing this stupid pink gown on the internet!" I shrieked.

"Since you guessed, I won't tell you."

Before I knew what I was doing, my fist had rammed straight into Emily's mouth, and my other had caught her in the stomach. She was on the floor gasping for breath, with blood trickling from the corner of her lips.

"Good grief!" Jenna exclaimed as she rushed into the room. "I leave you alone for five minutes and this happens." She surveyed the scene, "What did happen?"

It took another fifteen minutes to get everything straightened out and me cleaned up. The moment I had my belongings, I stormed out of the shop and began walking down Broadway. I'd seen a small café when we had come in, so I headed there. Pulling out my phone, I hit the selected number. "Hi. Mom? Can you please come get me?" My voice hitched then, and I just sank to my knees, leaning against the brick front of an office building.

Sobbing on my Mom's shoulder I relayed the whole event. Mom listened to everything, only taking a moment to call Emily's house to ensure that they had gotten in all right and that she was okay. While she talked to Mrs. DiMatteo, I simply hung my head in shame. I'd hit my best friend in the whole world.

The tears that streamed down my face couldn't begin to ease the distress that I was feeling. My world was crumbling around me. In the past week, I'd managed to alienate my best friend, and my own dog. Not a good track record.

"Well, I think I've got Betty calmed down. Emily is home, has a fat lip and some bruising. She told Betty almost the exact same story about what happened."

"Well, that's great!" I snarled through the tears. "She put a very embarrassing picture of me on the internet. It will be there forever. Maybe it's a good thing that I'm not doing well on solving this clue. I won't have to live with the embarrassment long."

"Stevie! I don't want to hear that kind of thing from you!"

I looked into her eyes; the tears were there just under the surface. "You're right. I'm sorry, Mom. It's just a bad situation, and I don't see it getting any better."

"Have you seen the picture?"

"No." I grabbed my phone from my purse and brought up Emily's FaceBook page. When I saw the picture, I cringed. I turned the phone to my mom, "Well, here it is. Wonderful huh? She's titled it 'Glamour Shot'."

CHAPTER 14

ENTROPY

Lying in my bed all day was as close to an escape hatch as I figured that I was going to find. Since the fiasco the day before, I hadn't talked to anyone not related by blood. Ian had tried to call, but I let it go directly to voice mail, Chris had texted, but I didn't respond. I figured that with everything that had happened over the past week, I was allowed to flake out for a few days and ignore the real world. At least until someone had the gumption to come in and strong arm me back into the general population.

So, since we had returned from church that morning, I had secluded myself in my room and was watching my ceiling fan revolve, lost in my own little thoughts. Some of these thoughts focused on how I was going to solve this clue and break the curse. I wondered how much I would be missed if things didn't work out. But, the most interesting thoughts I'd been having all morning were the ones devising a plan to get even with my best ex-friend, Emily.

Watching the fan make another series of rotations, I idly waved my fingers in front of my face trying to get the timing right so that I could make the fan appear to stop. I'd get it every once and a while, but nothing that I could maintain. Feeling disgusted with myself, and life in general, I rolled over and tried to read a novel.

Before this whole witch and curse thing had begun, I had been a voracious reader. Since September, I had only managed to read three books; two of which had been required for my English class.

Like most things in my life right now, the novel couldn't hold my interest for more than a few minutes. Again I turned my attention to the ceiling fan and thoughts of revenge.

My phone signaled a new text coming in, so I glanced at the screen. "What does she want now?" I asked the dolls that sat on the shelf. "She wants me to forgive her for sending that picture. What did it do to her? Nothing!" I tossed the phone to the other side of the bed and closed my eyes hoping for sleep to come.

Waking a few hours later, I decided that the sleep had done nothing to rid me of the depression that was still hanging over me. Maybe soaking in a hot tub would make things better.

Gathering my favorite bubble bath, and along with one of my favorite books, I plodded down the hall to the bathroom. I heard Kyle shut his door as I walked past, but I didn't think about it at all. For the next hour, I relaxed in the tub and let the tension begin to flow out.

I felt a little better, so I was pleased that I was finally turning the corner. Then, as I stood in front of the mirror, I noticed that sections of my hair were not it's normal color.

I leaned in closer. Instead of my mess of curly chestnut hair, there were streaks of almost white. But it was only where my hair had touched the water. I looked down; white there too! There was only one person who would even think to play such a dirty trick.

"Kyle!" I bellowed as I stormed out of the bathroom. As I swung through the doorway, I walked right into a layer of saran wrap that was covered with some thick, foul smelling stuff. The little jerk was standing there, just feet in front of me, laughing at me!

Killing him where he stood was not an option. Okay, it wasn't a good option. I screamed at the top of my lungs, "Mom! He ruined my hair!" Mom came up the stairs looked at the damage and laughed! The little twerp was going to escape from this with nothing.

"It's okay, Stevie, go take a shower then come on down and we'll see what we can do." And she walked away.

Looking right at him I said quietly, "You're going to pay for this, Kyle. I swear to you, I'm going to make you pay." He only snickered and retreated to his room.

Frustrated, I stomped back to the bathroom, tossed my now messed up robe into the hamper and got back into the tub for a much needed shower. Lost in the warm spray, my mind thought up revenge on the second person today. The big difference here was, I knew that I'd being seeing Kyle soon.

I was too caught up in my plans to notice that the white had washed out of my hair while I was back in the shower. I did however notice that his electric razor was sitting on the shelf. I quietly slid it into a folded towel, and carried everything back to my room.

Once in the safety of my room, I pulled out a set of tools that I used when the mood struck to make some very simple jewelry. Carefully, I unscrewed the backing plate and ran a few fine wires from the transformer to the screws. By leaving the screw heads up just slightly, both would make contact with Kyle's skin the next time he used this razor, and he should get a pretty good jolt from it.

I smiled in anticipation as I finished dressing and rushed back to the bathroom to replace the doctored razor. With a smile,

I set it back on the shelf and then worked on getting my hair brushed out.

Walking towards the stairs, I passed Kyle who was heading in to grab a shower and couldn't help smiling again. For once I was going to beat that brat.

I was talking with Mom in the kitchen when I heard the shower go on. The loud thud on the floor above startled both of us.

"Kyle?" Mom called up. There was no response other than the running shower.

Mom went to the stairs and called again, with similar results. When she headed up the stair, I didn't think anything of it. The scream that emanated form the bathroom made me jump.

"Scott! Come quick!"

Dad dropped the comics on the coffee table and headed up the stairs. I followed, wondering what the commotion was.

I stood in shock, my dad used his cell phone to call nine-one-one, and my mom had her hands over her mouth with tears streaming down her cheeks. Kyle lay, thankfully wrapped in his robe, unconscious on the bathroom floor. The razor lay in a small puddle, arcs of electricity flashing between the two exposed screws.

Two hours later, we were still seated in the emergency room. Kyle had woken up on the ambulance ride in, and the prognosis was good. He had suffered a concussion and an electrical burn. As soon as he had turned the razor on, he got zapped so bad that he'd jumped back and hit his head on the shelf knocking himself out. He had a bump on the back of his head where he had connected with the shelf, and two nasty looking burn marks on his hand.

As we waited for the doctors to finish running their series of test to determine the magnitude of the concussion, mom kept looking at me. Dad had gone to find some coffee and her staring got to the point that I had to know why.

"What?" I demanded.

"I'm trying to figure why you did this to you own brother," she said.

"Why are you blaming me?"

"Stevie, didn't you call me up when he played a harmless joke on you only an hour before?"

"Mom, he colored my hair! And nothing happened! I told you, and you walked away laughing about it."

"But electrocution, Stevie?"

I was beginning to lose it. "Why is it he can do anything to me, and he gets away with it scot free. Me? I do anything and I get clobbered for it! I'm tired of this! Look at my hair," I almost yelled, pulling it up to show the ends. "Look at what he did!"

"What did he do?"

Mom sat there pointing at my hair and I looked down. For the first time since I'd noticed the streaks in the mirror, I really looked at my hair. No streaks. A totally unruly mass of chestnut curls.

"What?" I spluttered. "There were white streaks before. You saw them," I was nearly hysterical now.

"He put a chemical in that coated your hair, making it appear white, Stevie. It rinsed out in the shower."

"Oh my God!" I bawled. "I could have killed him for it, and I nearly did!" Mom slid over next to me and held me as I cried. She was still holding me when Dad came back with coffees.

Grabbing a few cookies for comfort and courage, I walked towards my dad's home office later that night. I'd just left Kyle's room a few minutes earlier, and cried through my apology there. We were back on even footing there. So, now Kyle was upstairs resting, and would have a heck of a headache for the next few days according to the doctors. The burns on his hand, would take a while to heal, but should be better in about two weeks. However they would leave scars that he would carry for life. But we had both laughed about things before I left the room, so I felt a little better. But now I had to square things with my dad.

I knocked softly on the oak door, and heard my dad's weary voice, "Come in."

Pushing the door open, I ducked into the room. "Daddy?"

His head swiveled and fixed on me like he had missile lock. "What is it, Stevie?"

"I wanted to say, I'm sorry. I didn't mean for that to happen; it was supposed to be a harmless practical joke." I didn't even bother to try stopping the tears that flowed down my cheeks

"Well, it sure wasn't harmless. I can see by how you're reacting that you are feeling quite a bit of guilt here. That's good. You need to. I'm not going to tell you that you, actually both of you, have been warned that something was going to happen. Now that it did, there are consequences that must be paid."

"I've talked to Kyle already. I wish I could go back and not screw things up. Right now I'm so confused on so many things, that I just don't know what to do."

He smiled a little and motioned for me to come to him. When he pulled me close I sat on his lap and just let myself feel like I did when I was a little girl sitting here: safe and loved.

Crawling into bed that night, I burrowed into my covers, and wished that I could just make this weekend a bad memory. That there would be some way that when I went to school tomorrow, that Emily and I would still be friends. That something would have stopped me so I wouldn't have nearly killed my brother. But, in either case, my ego had pushed me to do things that I now regretted.

I thought about how my life had changed over the last few months. If someone had asked me, even a few weeks ago, I would have told them that my life couldn't have been much better. I'd gone from loner and outcast, to half of a couple. I had a few close friends that knew and understood me better than anyone else. I had a cute puppy that was there for me with a cold nose or wet kisses to cheer me up. Yeah, there was that stupid curse, but that was really the only down side of things.

Now, I'd lost my best friend. My dog wouldn't even be in the same room with me and my boyfriend was getting worried about me obsessing about this curse. I didn't think things could get much worse.

Trying to force yourself to go to sleep is often a wasted effort, and tonight was no exception. I looked around the room trying to find something that would occupy my mind and let it turn off enough to let me sleep. The answer came when I saw a book that my dad's sister Nancy had given me when I had been going through a bad time several years ago while I was recovering from a car accident.

Aunt Nancy and I had gone to New York City to see a matinee of *Wicked* and had had a great time. After stopping for pizza we headed home, laughing and enjoying each other's company. That's when the drunk driver hit us. I had multiple broken bones and needed months to learn how to walk again.

I had always looked up to Aunt Nancy, for her courage and determination. Even though she had been paralyzed from the waist down in the accident, she never gave up or lost her can do attitude. When she had seen me struggling, she gave me a book of encouraging quotes.

On nights like tonight, when it seemed that the whole world was crashing in on my head, I would often sit and read that book. So far, it had never failed to give me the courage I needed to push on.

Opening the book, I started reading the quotes softly to myself. When my door creaked open, I looked and the waterworks started as Misty jumped up onto my bed.

CHAPTER 15

DEFECTION

Walking to the bus stop on Monday was a new experience. It was the first time since I started school that Emily and I hadn't made the trip together. The hardest part wound up being the stares that I had to endure when I got to the corner. Emily was talking with a girl that I didn't know and kept glaring at me over her shoulder. As I moved towards the edge of the crowd, they repositioned themselves closer to the middle. It didn't give me any sort of warm fuzzy feeling.

I looked over the assembled group, hoping that Chris would be here. I guess I really wanted to talk to someone today, but who? Another glance around, and I noticed that everyone here was staring at me, and I could only guess, but I was pretty sure that I was also the topic of most of the conversations. This was going to be a long day for sure.

Knowing that you are about to spend an entire day being shunned by almost the entire school isn't exactly new to me. I've been a loner most of my life, choosing to have only a small group of friends that really knew me. Today however, even that close group was trying to figure out what I had done. As the bus rambled on towards the village, I tried to look around to find Emily. Maybe if I could talk to her, we could get things straightened out.

She was currently sitting in the front of the bus with the same girl she had been talking to at the stop. I had ended up in one of the rear seats, directly over the tire wells. So I rode in silence, with my knees tucked almost up to my chin, thinking about what I'd like to say.

As soon as the bus came to a stop at the far end of the loop, I stood up hoping to make a break for it and get to the exit before Emily had a chance to escape. My incredible luck was working overtime today. No sooner had I stood up, when Mrs. Kattz started to move again. I found myself tumbling head over heels towards the back of the bus. Everyone laughed at my improvised gymnastics.

By the time the bus had reached the part of the loop nearest the building and the door whooshed open, I was lying flat on my stomach in a puddle of who knows what and the rest of the riders were already filing out, stepping on me as they went.

Quietly, I slipped off of the bus and made my way around the edge of the school to the gym doors. These doors weren't used frequently during the day as they were too far from the student lot and the bus loop. Today, I was craving the alone time.

I slipped into the gym locker room, and rummaged through the stack of clothes that I kept there. I'd like to say that this morning's occurrence on the bus was an unusual event, but I seem to be so accident prone, I'd decided when I was in elementary school that it paid to keep an entire outfit at school for just such occasions.

I pulled off the now salt-stained blouse that I'd chosen so carefully, and replaced it with a simple tee shirt. Once I'd finished, I leaned against the lockers tying to get up the courage to walk out and face the day.

I heard the warning bell ring, signaling that I had five minutes to get to my homeroom. Sighing, I picked up my backpack and the gym bag that was now filled with my dirty clothes and headed for the door.

Hoping that I would be able to circumvent the vast majority of the school's population, I headed for the back stairs that would end just a few feet from my locker. Checking to see if the coast was clear, I cautiously moved into the hall and rushed to my locker. I really didn't want to have a run in or a stare down with Emily right now if I was going to beat the tardy bell.

I fumbled with my combination, and actually had to stop and command myself to take a series of deep breaths before I could get it opened.

Dumping my gym bag on the floor inside, I hung my coat on the peg and grabbed the books that I was going to need for the first few classes. Slamming the locker closed, I rushed towards Mrs. Vallente's room.

As I turned the corner, right outside her room, I literally ran into Brian Kellan. Our notebooks flew in every possible direction, and papers rained down like huge snowflakes. Since Brian outweighs me by a considerable margin, I found myself flat on my back as a result of our unexpected meeting.

"Sorry about that," he said in a genuinely pleasant voice. "Let me give you a hand up."

The bell sounded just as I took his hand and was pulled to my feet. "Thanks. Are you okay, Brian?"

"Hey no problem. I have some extra padding so things just bounce off of me." He shot me a quick grin as he picked up his one book and headed off to his homeroom.

I began gathering my things, when Mrs. Vallente walked out of the room. "A little late today, Stevie?"

"Sorry, I sort of bumped into Brian."

"Well, get your stuff together, and clear the hall before we head to first period." She ducked back into her room, leaving me stuffing papers back into my bag. I was almost done when the bell rang and the halls were filled with noisy chatter of students heading into their classes.

Ian came up from behind me and touched me on the elbow. I nearly jumped out of my skin. "Little jumpy are we, Stevie?" He smiled at my frustrated expression.

"Sorry, Ian. It's just been one of those mornings. It seems that if it could go wrong, that it has."

"Like what?" he asked as he grabbed my hand and started leading me towards orchestra.

"Well, lets see. It's only eight oh-five in the morning, and I've picked myself up off of two different floors. Only one required a complete change of clothes."

"Now see? That's a good thing. It went in your favor."

"Oh, I'm just warming up. How about the fact that Emily and I haven't spoken to each other since Saturday morning? When I saw her this morning at the bus, she kept avoiding me. It's awful hard to make amends with people when they are avoiding being near you."

"Well, you did punch her out on Saturday. I'd be a little wary of your right hook too if I'd been on the receiving end of it once already."

"Not helping, Ian. It's got me all screwed up. Worse than normal." We were now just outside the orchestra room.

He stopped us, pulled me around so we were facing each other and he lifted my chin. "Stevie, I know that right now this all seems like the end of the world, but it really is only a little blip in the grand scheme. Trust me on this. I'll talk to Emily and see if I can speed things up a bit." His kiss left me standing in the door to the music room looking stunned.

Orchestra wasn't too bad. Everybody was too absorbed in the music to spend too much time gossiping. But even here, I could see the stares and whispered conversations. By the time I was on my way to gym the rest of the student population wasn't even trying to hide things. Every hallway I walked down, the eyes followed me and I could hear the comments "…that's her. She's the one who freaked out and knocked out her best friend…"

I rushed into the locker room, and headed right for one of the bathroom stalls. Once there, I just sat on the toilet, doubled over clasping my stomach and fought the urge to either let my anger or my tears loose. Neither was going to help with my current situation.

Heat balled in my stomach, I tried to ignore it, but it became too much. Quickly jumping to my feet and spinning around I vomited into the toilet with a loud retching noise. I lost control of all of my emotions, and the tears that I'd fought to keep back rushed to the surface.

Wiping my mouth, it occurred to me that I'd cried more in the last six months than I had over the past five years. I wanted to cry about that, but I just couldn't let it keep getting to me.

I'd heard the din of the other girls quiet, so I carefully opened the door and peered out. As far as I could tell, there was no one in sight. I walked to my locker and began dressing for gym as Mrs. Phelps walked in.

"Not feeling too well today, eh, Champ?"

I looked at her, too upset to care if my look of disgust got me in trouble. "I'm fine. Just had a bit of nausea."

"If you're sure, then get dressed."

I finished dressing, wondering why I hadn't taken the easy way out and gone to the nurse and eventually home. Oh, yeah. That's right: I'm not too bright.

French proved to be the worst class thus far. With Emily right in the class, everybody took sides; or more precisely her side. It made it very hard to get over to talk to her when every time I made a move in that direction, I had eighteen other students blocking my way.

I kept looking over towards her, hoping that my expression would transmit my apology to her. Maybe if she saw it, she'd come over to me and we could start to talk this out.

I felt my phone vibrate, and slowly slid it out to peek at the text. Since phones aren't allowed in class, I had to be careful to do it only when Madame Lynn had her back to me. It took nearly five minutes before I was able to extract my phone and glance at the screen. Emily had sent me a text! Maybe this would be the opening that I was craving. I clicked on it, and read.

STOP LOOKING AT ME & DROP DEAD!

Entering the cafeteria I wasn't really hungry. To be honest, I don't think I could have eaten anyway. I began making my way towards my normal table, but stopped when I saw Emily already sitting there. The girl from this morning was there too, and it looked like Emily was busy trying to get other people to fill in the seats.

Sighing, I decided that I would just get a drink and sit outside on the steps by the courtyard. Pulling my legs up to minimize the area exposed to the cold March air, I leaned my head back and tried to clear my mind and think.

Regardless of how Emily and I were doing, I still had to solve the clue by the equinox. Just more than a week left. I really hoped that Emily and I could make up by then so that if things didn't work out she wouldn't be left remembering that our last words had been harsh.

I heard the door open behind me, and cursed my luck. I had wanted to be alone to sulk, but it looked like I'd have company. I decided that I'd ignore whoever it was. It was a big set of steps, and we could sit in companionable silence. Then I felt the jacket being draped over me. I opened my eyes to glare.

"You looked cold," Ian shrugged. "Figured this would help a bit."

"I'm not good company right now, Ian. I've tried to talk to her several times today, and the only communications she has had with me was to tell me to drop dead! What am I going to do? I'm coming apart at the seams and it doesn't seem that there is anyway to stop it."

He sat next to me, draped his arm around my shoulder and just held me.

Why is it that I can be in such a foul mood one minute, and then thirty seconds after he shows up, all it takes is a firm embrace and I'm back on steady ground? I swear that there are days that I think he is part wizard or something. Today was no exception: he sat down, pulled me in and my worries went away. Two minutes later, I wasn't angry or upset. I was turned on.

"I talked to Emily before I came out here. She needs time right now. I think she is hurting as much as you, but doesn't know how to handle things."

I looked over at him, "And I do? She's been my best friend for twelve years, and now we aren't speaking. It's killing me."

"Give her the time she needs. It will probably take less than a week, but you guys will be all right again."

"I may only have a week. The equinox is coming up fast. I'm scared of so many things right now."

"Relax. It'll be okay. Just calm yourself now."

"Ian, what am I going to do? She's in my history class next period, and we sit next to each other."

"She called her mom. She'll be leaving right after lunch, so you should be clear there today."

I wasn't sure how I felt about this. Part of me was relieved that I didn't have to do this today, but part was scared of putting it off.

History did have a surprise for me. It wasn't who was absent, but rather who wanted to talk to me.

"Hey, Stevie," Gabby said unsure of how I was going to react. "I know that you've had a rough day today. I wanted to let you know that I understand how you're feeling."

"Thanks, Gabby, I think. I'm not sure you can really know how I feel, but I'll take just about any kind of sympathy I can get today."

"I can get behind that. Listen, after school today, why don't you let Tanya and I buy you a cup of coffee. You can just vent and know that whatever you say won't hurt feelings between us."

I must have been really drained. "Yeah, that sounds nice."

Stirring my cup of tea that afternoon, I sat in a booth and voluntarily talked to Gabby and Tanya. Maybe they weren't so bad after all. I listened to them recount an episode that they had had back when we were all in seventh grade. I vaguely remembered the scene. I could feel myself starting to relax slightly and felt sluggish despite the caffeine in the tea.

"So, what is really going on between you and my cousin?" Gabby wanted to know.

I laughed. "We're dating each other; enjoying each other's company. Right now he's been the only person that has been able to keep me steady with everything that has been going on."

Tanya winked across the table at Gabby. "I can see that. He always struck me as a stuck-up-do-gooder from the few times I ran into him. But, I think he'd be good and steady during a friendly upheaval."

"Yeah, he's been helpful trying to help with this family problem that I've been dealing with for the last few months, the problem with Emily. Add in Chrissy's problem, and Ian's had his hands full these past few months."

"Who is Chrissy?" Gabby asked suddenly interested in the conversation.

My mind was sounding the little alarm bells, but before I could control it I blurted out, "Chrissy Lehr. She's having some serious issues." My hand slapped across my mouth. "Whoops! That's supposed to be a secret."

"Oh, don't worry. We won't tell anyone," Tanya said with a smile. With a nod to Gabby, they got up dropped a few bills on the table and left.

Alone at the table, I sat and wondered what had just happened. When I moved my cup away from me, I saw the two parts of the capsule rolling around.

"Oh no," I muttered. I pulled out my phone and called the only person that I felt I could trust right now. "Ian. I think your cousin slipped me some kind of drug."

CHAPTER 16

RINSE AND REPEAT

Nightmares, both real and imagined, disturbed my sleep that night. I lay awake, tossing and turning, thinking about the secret that I had divulged. Granted, one of the two had slipped me something, but that didn't change the fact that I had let Chrissy's secret out.

When I called Chris, after everything had worn off, and explained what had happened he went ballistic. Not that I could argue. He was still fighting with Mark, so his home life was shaky grounds. Having this news get out could very well be the straw that breaks the camel's back.

On the rare occasions that I did doze off, I seemed to be almost instantly transported to the clearing with the witch. She was growing more excited as the time to the equinox drew closer.

I found myself exhausted, wishing for sleep but dreading the idea of sleep. It was a precarious catch twenty-two.

When I opened my eyes this last time, I could see the beginning of sunrise lighting the sky. My room was still dark and unusually cold, emphasized by Misty's cold nose, which was now pressing into a bare spot on my back.

Crawling out of bed was a new form of torture; it wasn't cold in my room, it was freezing. "What the heck?" I asked the pile of covers. I could see my breath.

Huddling into my robe, I tried to make it to the door. Every joint in my body was screaming out in protest. Shuffling to the door, I tried to pull it open. It was locked. "This can't be happening. This door is never locked," I nearly cried. I yanked on the knob; nothing. Giving up, I banged on the door.

"Stevie, what's all the banging for?" Mom asked.

"Mom, there's something wrong with my door. It won't open." I heard the knob rattle.

"Hmmm. I'm going to get your dad. He'll figure this out."

Ten minutes later, I was still locked in my room, shivering, while the rest of the family stood outside trying to find a way to get me out. I was starting to lose feeling in my feet, when an idea struck. "Dad," I called through the door. "If I take the hinges off the door, it should be able to be opened, locked or not, correct?"

"Probably," came his reply.

"Okay then, I'm going to give it a try."

I grabbed the screwdriver from my kit I used for making jewelry, and began to pry the hinge pins. It took fifteen more minutes, but finally the hinges were out, and the door swung open in a cross between an arc and a tumble and hit me square in the head.

Getting to school turned out to be almost the same as yesterday, except I was able to avoid the falling down on the bus and in the hallways. Groups of students lingered at their lockers, watching me pass. Their stares made me feel like a leper. The few times that I did see Emily, she reacted the same way as yesterday.

I was truly beginning to feel that what had happened between us on Saturday was going to destroy our friendship. Realizing this loss was overwhelming. I did whatever I could to put it out of my mind and get through the rest of what I had to do.

Perhaps, if I were real lucky, I'd find a way to solve this clue and live long enough to make amends. I didn't want to think about the possibility of eternity with this rift hanging over my head. It was too much to bear.

Stepping into my French class that day was going to take almost all of my strength. What I really wanted to do was to run to the nurse's office and fake an illness. Not a real responsible reaction, but at least it would give me some distance between

Emily and myself. I hadn't realized that I'd actually stopped just outside of the door until one of the other students pushed by me.

"Stevie?" Emily's voice was shaky and nervous.

I turned cautiously. Her usually vivid blue eyes were now puffy and red. I wanted to speak, but my mouth wasn't engaging.

"I'm so sorry, Stevie." Tears began streaming down her face.

Whatever it was that was freezing me to that space melted instantly. I grabbed her in a fierce hug and held on while my tears joined hers.

"Em, I didn't mean to hit you. I just lost my…"

"I deserved it. Posting that picture was stupid and now I have to live with what it did; whatever it caused."

"Can we be friends again?"

"God, I thought you'd hate me forever," she said as tears again fell on her cheeks.

It felt good to at least have one of my friends back. As we went into the room, I told her briefly about what had happened with Tanya and Gabby yesterday.

"I guess I really screwed things up. If you'd voluntarily go with those two."

"To say that I was a mess, well that would be an understatement. And look where it got me. Dropped me into another case of bad judgment. I've been trying to talk to Chris all day, but he's been ignoring me. It's been real lonely."

Emily reached over, squeezed my hand. "We'll all get through this."

After class, I walked with Emily to our lockers before heading to lunch. Many of the students who had been glaring at me earlier were now looking at us with a puzzled look. Seeing Emily beside me, they finally smiled and waved at me. It felt like a weight had been lifted and I was being let back into the general population.

Turning the corner into the café, we were too engrossed in our own conversation to notice the atmosphere that was brewing. Reaching our table, I dropped into a chair, and then noticed the stares. They weren't looking at me, or so it seemed. It appeared that they were looking at our entire table. Once again, we were the standouts. We tried to ignore them, but I kept getting these little tickles on the back of my neck.

"What's going on with everybody?" Ian asked. Okay, so, he's noticed it too.

"I dunno. They keep looking over here; almost like they are waiting for something to happen," Emily casually remarked.

I glanced up, as I saw a movement out of the corner of my eye. Chris had entered the room, but then left the same way that he'd come from. "I've got a feeling that I'm somehow at the center of this again. Em and I having our little disagreement, and then they way I screwed up with Chris. He saw me and just walked out."

"Darn," Emily spat, dropping her sandwich. She stood up. "I'll see if I can find him and talk to him."

"I've really stepped into it this time, haven't I?"

Ian swallowed before answering. "You've been juggling a lot recently. Your emotions are almost raw, so it doesn't take much to get you to explode. Unfortunately, my cousin and her accomplice used that to exploit you yesterday."

"Ian, I feel so bad. You know that I never would have broken Chris' confidence like that. I failed him, I..."

"Stevie," his had now rested on mine. "Gabby used a drug to get you to relax so that she could pump you for information. To be honest, I think that many people have noticed signs with Chris, but they don't know the whole story."

"They didn't until I opened my mouth yesterday."

"No one can blame you for what happened."

I sat there, leaving my lunch untouched and looked longingly at the door. The feeling of wanting to get out of here was strengthening. The only reason that I didn't leave was that Emily and Chris walked in and headed over to our table.

Watching Chris walk towards me, I could easily see the anger just under the surface. There was something else there as well, but it wasn't as obvious. The dark circles under his eyes spoke volumes of how little sleep he'd gotten last night.

"Chris," I said as he pulled out a chair. "I'm so—"

"Stuff your apology, Stevie. I know that you went out with those two yesterday, and that you wanted to talk to them. I really thought that you'd keep my situation in confidence."

"Chris, they put something in my drink. I wasn't aware of what I was doing after that. I can't tell you how badly I feel right now."

He glared across the table at me for a full thirty seconds. "I guess it was going to come out anyway, but I just wish that I'd been able to have a little more say in when and where," he let out a long sigh. "I'm scared."

"What did I miss?" Ian asked.

"We were just…" I broke off noticing the pair of spectators. I moved closer to Ian, so that my back was now to the two uninvited onlookers who were now watching us, "Gabby and Tanya are standing on the other side of that table," I motioned with a slight jerk of my head. "They're standing there trying to figure out what is going on. Chris is getting concerned."

Ian set his tray down, "I'm going to go talk to my cousin. I'll be right back," he announced and turned towards the two girls.

I sat next to Chris, rubbing my hand on his back. He was feeling the pressure of this issue right now, and I'm the one who inadvertently set the cross hairs on him. "It'll be okay," I tried to assure him.

I saw the smirk on Gabby's face as Ian approached. They were far enough away that I could not hear what was being said, but I could tell by their body language that it wasn't a simple greeting. When Tanya burst into a laugh, at the same time Gabby turned beet red, I guessed that Ian was fighting blackmail with blackmail.

I've heard the expression, 'it's all fair in love and war', before but this is the first time that I've ever thought that there could be real casualties involved. I just hoped that whatever Ian was doing wasn't going to come back and bite us hard.

Gossip was flowing in the halls as we left the café and headed to our next class. Depending on who was talking depended on what was being said. On the walk to my English class, I heard everything from Chris was supposedly gay and dating Ian, making me the beard, to Chris supposedly having flower tattoos all over his body. It seemed that the longer things went on, the crazier the story became.

I truly wished that there were someway for Chris to suddenly jump to June, so this phase of life would be over and he could transition or whatever he needed to do. I hated the fact that if I hadn't lost control, even for a minute, his secret wouldn't be anywhere on the school population's radar.

Passing by a bank of lockers just outside of Ms. Daily's room right after English I saw the biggest clique in the school having what looked like a club meeting. This group was full of all of the most popular kids, all of whom considered anyone who wasn't like them as being unworthy.

It was while I was walking that I heard the first rumor that scared me. They wanted to corner Chris and force him to divulge his secret and put an end to all of the gossip that everyone else was feeding.

In class, I deftly palmed my phone out of my pocket and texted Chris and Ian what I had just heard. I could only hope that with a little advance warning, they would be able to ward off any problems before they got out of hand.

Laying my head down on my desk, I tried to ignore the whispers that were going on around me. Obviously, my classmates were hoping that I would get sucked into the gossip and spill what I knew. The more that they talked, the more I worked to ignore them. Instead, I concentrated on remembering the lyrics to a specific song, hoping that Mrs. Vallente would get the class started before things got out of control.

Mrs. Vallente rushed into the room right at the bell. Her face was a bit flush, as if she'd been running or something. "Sorry that I'm almost late," she said with a grin. "But there was a little situation out in the hall that I needed to help with." She turned to the computer for her PowerPoint presentation, and proceeded to keep us busy until the end of the period.

Anxiety had me on pins and needles. I hadn't received any confirmation from either Chris or Ian that they had gotten the message, so I didn't know if Chris was okay or not right now. I figured since I hadn't heard any sirens, that at least he didn't need medical attention. I tried not to think of any other possibility.

When the bell finally rang, instead of heading to Mr. Sweeny's room, I headed in the direction of Chris's last class of the day. As I got closer, I noticed a large group forming around the gym doors. My heart sank. I didn't need to ask; I knew what had happened. The clique had gotten to Chris.

I felt like I was going to throw up, and in a moment of cowardice, I ran to the nurse's office, bolting past the secretary and into the private bathroom, where I was violently ill.

CHAPTER 17:

FALLOUT

Throwing up is not dignified, regardless of where you are spewing. Doing it at school is probably about the worst place that I can think of to be throwing up. But, there I sat, curled up in a ball on the bathroom floor in the nurse's office.

Anything that I had had in my system was now speeding into the sewer system, and I was exhausted. I let my head drop back against the cool tiles of the wall and closed my eyes.

The sudden knock startled me, "Ms. Nixon," Mrs. Murphy called. "Are you still sick?"

"I think I'm done." For now, at least, I promised myself.

"Who would you like me to call for you?"

"Um, no one actually. I'll be fine in a few minutes." I heard the muffled ring of the telephone, and the click of her heels as she retreated to answer.

In the silence, I wondered about the lies that I'd just told her. Was I still sick? Oh yeah. No questions there. I was sick to my stomach with just the thought of what had happened to Chris. I was sick of how people in my school reacted to things that were different from what they were. And I was sick of beating myself up about feeling guilty of how Gabby and Tanya had used me to get the dirt on Chris.

Yeah, I was sick, but not as sick as some of the people who were leading this group.

I heard the door click open and a hand take hold of my elbow and give a tug. I looked up to see that Emily was standing there. "Come on," she said. "Lets get you cleaned up and we can go find the others."

I let her pull me up and took a long look in the mirror. "I look like something the cat dragged in," I whispered in horror.

"Let me see," Emily said as she pulled out her ever-ready bag of cosmetics. Two minutes later, I didn't exactly look like myself, but I was at least presentable. Heading to the door, we passed Mrs. Murphy. I waved, "Thanks for letting me use the bathroom."

"Are you sure that you feel okay to go back? Would you rather I call your mom and have her come get you?"

"Mrs. Murphy, really I'm fine. I've just got a lot that is on my plate right now."

"If you even feel a little sick, I want you back in here. Got it?" she asked with a stern smile.

"Yes, ma'am." I replied as we headed out the door.

"Where are we going?" I asked as Emily kept her hand on my arm and led me away from the area near the gym.

"Ian managed to get Chris out before anything super-serious happened, but right now we are meeting in Lerch's office"

I swallowed hard. I was angry with myself for my lack of control yesterday, now I was feeling even guiltier knowing that Chris may have been hurt. "How is Chris?"

Emily shrugged. "I'm not sure. Like I said, Ian was able to get Chris out before things got too out of hand. From what little I saw of Chris, I didn't see any blood, but that doesn't mean much."

Walking to the principal's office was becoming a habit. An unwelcomed habit. Emily's phone chirped, and she pulled it out to look at the text. "Ian is meeting us at the office."

"Good. Did he say how Chris is?"

"No, but I'm asking him now," she said as her thumbs raced over the keyboard. "Hopefully he'll have something that will put us both at ease."

"That would be nice," I agreed. We walked for another couple of seconds in silence. Turning the corner to the main corridor, I spied two police cruisers pulling in. "This doesn't bode well," I mumbled while pointing to the cars.

"Maybe," Emily sighed. "Although, I wouldn't exactly object if they are arresting the people who are responsible for doing this to Chris."

"I'd agree to that."

"Emily!" a voice rang from the stair well. We turned around to see who was calling.

Dee raced down the last few steps and hurried to join up with us. "Is it true? The rumor about Chris getting stabbed?"

"Stabbed?" I gasped. I had a whole new image in my mind of what might have happened.

"I don't think so, Dee. We were just in the nurse's office. If someone had gotten really hurt, I don't think she would have been hovering over Stevie. Mrs. Murphy would have been doing triage or whatever for the injured party."

The three of us were now walking together in a line that had Emily in the middle. I was glad that she was there to do most of the talking to Dee. My mind was too occupied talking myself out of the idea of running out of the building, waving my arms and screaming like a mad woman.

As we neared the office, Dee stopped at her locker. While fussing with the combination she said, "I really hope Chris is okay. It's sad don't you think? The way people treat each other."

We nodded and made our way to the office door.

Opening the door, we walked into the main part of the office. Mrs. Croft sat behind her desk, her fingers clicking away at the keyboard. Ian was pacing the small waiting area like a big cat.

"Ian, what do you know about Chris? Is he okay?" I asked as I flung myself into his arms. I needed the comfort of the embrace more than I realized.

"I think he's okay. When I got your text, I decided to detour on my way to art, and saw Chris enter into the locker room. I went in, only half a minute behind, but they were already on him. When I shouted, they took off, but much of the damage was already done."

"What's going on now?' Emily asked.

"Right now, Mrs. Lerch, Mr. Bigelow and someone I don't know are meeting with a couple of cops. From what I gather, they are going to want to talk to us about what we know. "

I heard the click of the door, and braced myself for whatever laid behind it.

Hearing the voices that were coming from behind the door sent my stomach into another round of nausea. The panic attack that I had experienced in the nurse's office began to pale to what I felt right this moment.

"Stevie," Ian said calmly, "relax. It's going to be fine."

"Huh?"

"Your hand went cold as ice, and you are pure white. Breathe, relax and don't worry about this."

"Easy for you to say. You're not the one who spilled everything that caused this problem."

"The information that you, as you called it, spilled wasn't the root of this issue. We have people who are willing to listen now, and hopefully will do so objectively."

He tugged my hand in order to get me moving again. Slowly we entered into Mrs. Lerch's office, with Emily following right behind.

"Ah, Sheriff Guliano," Mrs. Lerch began and motioned towards us. "These are Stevie Nixon, Ian Morris, and Emily DiMatteo. They are all friends of Chris Lehr. These," she said pointing to the other adults in the room, "are Sheriff Guliano, Officer Addams, and the school psychologist, Doctor Reidy. Please, take a seat."

Mrs. Lerch sat on the small couch that ran along the wall and took a sip of water. "I know that you three are all concerned about what is going on right now. Let me assure you that you are not in any trouble, and that we are trying to get to the bottom of this unfortunate incident. Sheriff Guliano? You've got the floor."

I turned to look at the sheriff. He looked to be about the same age as my dad, but was huskier. His skin was the same color as light caramel, and his tight black hair was shaved so that you could actually see his scalp. His eyes caught me, and the way that he looked at me indicated that he was going to be a no-nonsense type of guy. Perfect, I thought. He appeared to be just the kind of person that I wanted working this case.

"As Mrs. Lerch has already said, I'm Sheriff Andy Guliano, and I'm in charge of finding out what happened to your friend. I'm very sorry that he was hurt, but now I need you to give me a run down on what is going on. What you observed, what you think, and in general catch me up to speed on what's happening here at Sleepy Hollow High. Who'd like to start?"

Closing my eyes, I took a deep breath and started to tell the story. The room was quiet for the most part as I took them through how I'd been the one to divulge my friend's secret. How I now loathed myself for the momentary lapse of reason, regardless of why it happened. The truth of the matter was, if I hadn't slipped up with Tanya and Gabby, no one from outside of our group would have known about Chris.

When I finished, I let my head hang down in shame. I heard a soft sound coming from next to me, but it wasn't Ian. When I opened my eyes, Officer Addams was right there.

"It's okay, Stevie. You didn't even stand a chance of keeping that secret. As soon as they put that drug into your system, it was as if you'd wanted to tell them everything. It's not a matter of you having a lapse of reason that caused you to tell Chris's secret. No, it was a case of two manipulators working together to take advantage of you.

Pausing to confer with the sheriff and the psychologist, Officer Addams had taken on the role of 'good-cop' during our session. I was pretty sure that this wasn't a role that he took out of the closet on certain days, but who he really was. As the adults conferred in the corner working out the report, I studied Addams.

He was an imposing man, over six feet, but the wide shoulders gave way to a trim waist that made me think of a serious athlete, probably football. He was clean-shaven, and his short black hair was closely cropped, but not as short as Guliano's. Maybe it was his eyes that gave me reason to pause; they appeared to be able to look right through you. In honesty, they freaked me out a bit.

While they were talking, Emily, Ian and I just sat quietly. Each of us lost in our own personal thoughts. I occasionally noticed Ian looking at me. His expression was querying me about how I felt. I simply answered his look with a shrug, simple and non-committal.

Trying to be respectful of what they were doing, I finally broke the silence between the three of us. "Any idea on what's going on?" I asked quietly.

Ian shrugged. "From what I've observed here, there might be enough for this to actually be considered a hate crime, but that's not a given. And of course, there is the matter of who's word do you believe? I'm fairly sure that Tony isn't going to be singing out about taking down someone like Chris."

I wish we had more info on how Chris is doing," Emily stated.

"Yeah that would be nice, " I agreed. "Do you guys think that there is anything else that we can do to stop this?"

"I think that the group that you are supposed to be starting with Mrs. Vallente will go a long way in starting to affect change."

"I'd forgotten about working on that. I've been too tied up with the, um, other stuff, that I haven't made the time to work on it.

Waiting is not something that I do very well. I have patience, just not much. Waiting today gave me way too much time to think about things. I mean, being introspective is good, but there comes a point where you become obsessive and rethink every little thing you've done. I was afraid that I was rapidly closing in on that point as I sat in that office.

Ian must have sensed something, as he took my hand and gave it a light squeeze. When I looked over at him, he just gave me a comforting smile.

"Okay," Mrs. Lerch said as she and the other adults came back over to our side of the room. "From the statements that each of you made, we've been able to get a basic picture of what happened. Mr. Bigelow is going to take Officer Addams to the IT room so that they can go over the videos from the halls. This should give us corroborating evidence, which should allow us to delve further into this fiasco."

After Mr. Bigelow and Officer Addams left, Mrs. Lerch began again. "I know that each of you is anxiously awaiting to hear how your friend is doing. The last I heard, Mr.Pratt had treated him in the gym office with some ice packs. There doesn't appear to be any serious injuries, but he did take a few blows. He has been taken to the hospital to have a thorough exam, and is currently under police protection."

"What's going to happen to the kids that were involved?" I asked.

"Well, Stevie, that's going to be a two part answer. Part one, is how things will be handled here at the school. If we can get one member of the group to break and give us the names of everyone that was involved, all of them will be suspended. The second part will be through the Sheriff's office."

"But I gave you all of the names," Ian stated. "What's the delay?"

"Mrs. Lerch rolled her eyes, and glanced over at Sheriff Guliano. "I'm sure that you have all heard the saying, 'innocent until proven guilty'?" We all nodded. She continued, "In this case, we have no direct proof of who was involved—yet. Ian, you gave us a series of names. I know that you were there because Mr. Pratt saw you go in, heard the yelling and then you came out carrying Chris. What we have to do is let the system work. The sheriff and I will be talking to these boys individually. I think between the two of us, we will be able to break at least one of them. Once that happens, we just roll them on each other."

"What if they stick together, you know, give each other alibis?" Emily asked.

Sheriff Guliano answered this one. "One of the things that is happening as we speak, is that one of my crime lab techs will be gathering Chris's clothes and taking pictures of his injuries. If we can't get one of the people that you named to break for us, we'll just take things up one step. It'll be a bit more difficult since we are working with minors, but we will get DNA samples as well as fist impressions, and possibly shoe impressions. The lab boys will do their magic, and we'll have some solid evidence to go on. The down side of that is the time that will be involved. Unlike CSI on TV, it takes awhile for results to come in."

"How much time?" I asked.

"Well, if we processed the clothes today, it might take us one to two days to get the samples ready to be run. DNA tests will take anywhere from two to four days. We might have better luck running and matching the prints, but I won't know that until later."

"What happens once you get these guys?" I asked the sheriff.

"If we get them to come clean on their own, the school will handle most of the actual punishment. Yes, there would be charges filed, but because they'd turned themselves in, the charges would most likely be reduced and they would get probation."

"If, however, they make us go through all the work and effort, they won't have a chance to plea it down, and we get to add a few charges. They could conceivably be looking at anywhere from six months to ten years of jail time. Perhaps more if the evidence warrants a charge of attempted murder."

The phone on Mrs. Lerch's desk rang, and after a brief discussion, she turned to us, "Your folks are here now. They will be taking you to the hospital to be with your friend now."

CHAPTER 18

DISGRACED

Walking into the Emergency room at the hospital we saw a number of people huddled around Chris' parents. There were some friends, and a uniformed police officer was standing a few feet back. The entire group was quiet, as if they were afraid that saying anything would bring the doctors out with bad news.

Ian caught up with me, and we walked over together. "Mrs. Brown?" I asked timidly feeling rude intruding on this private time for her.

Her eyes came up wearily and rested on my face. "Oh, Stevie," she gushed as the tears started to fall again. I bent down and hugged her. "He's doing well, so they tell me," she choked out.

Hearing that he was doing well was a relief. If the doctors said it, it must be true. That's how I'd gotten myself through after my long ago accident. I had to believe it. "I'm so sorry. If I'd been…"

"Stevie, it's okay," she said. "I know that you'd never intentionally hurt him." She pushed away a little so she could look me in the face. "It was a comfort for him to know that you knew about Chrissy. It's something that we all have been dealing with, and keeping it internalized has caused so many problems these past few months."

I glanced over at Mark, who had a look of distain on his face. I knew what she said was at least partially true; it had caused grief between Chris and the rest of the family. But I wondered if Chris would still be glad that I knew about it?

I stared out the window as the Browns talked to Ian, Mrs. Brown repeatedly kissing him for what he had done for Chris. I let my mind wander slightly. Here we were closing in on the middle of March, and I still hadn't solved the clue. I had no idea where exactly we stood on any of it.

My friends had helped me through a great deal of difficulties with this whole quest, but right now I felt hopelessly alone. One of my closest friends was lying in a bed somewhere in this emergency ward because of my actions. What if my actions of working on this clue caused one of them serious harm?

My mind quickly brought the picture of Emily's close encounter to the forefront. They had volunteered to help me solve this, but they hadn't bargained to have their lives on the line with mine. I was going to need to find some down time in the very near future to see if I could resolve this. Somehow, and I didn't know how yet, I was going to have to find a way to solve this blasted riddle while keeping my friends safe at the same time.

Shouts sounded in the hallway. I looked around and noticed that the Browns were gone and that the officer who had been standing back was now racing down the hall. "Oh, God! Chris!" I nearly shrieked. I felt several firm hands grip me; Ian was standing in front of me holding my hands while my dad had come over behind me and had his hands on my shoulders. Of course neither of them was holding me up, so when I blacked out, I simply slid to the floor.

I woke to find myself lying on a gurney being wheeled down the hall. Glancing to the side I saw two nurses guiding the gurney along the way. "What happened? Where are you taking me?"

"Ah good, you've come to. You apparently fainted, but according to your dad, you hit your head pretty hard on the corner of the couch in the waiting room. We'll have you stitched up and out of x-ray before you know it," the young Asian nurse on my left said.

I was wheeled into a small room. I could see the Brown's standing outside the door across the way, so I could only guess that is where Chris was. Minutes later, a young doctor came in, and after a quick shot of Novocain, he proceeded to stitch me up. As soon as he left, an orderly arrived to escort me to x-ray.

As I expected, it was just another bump on my unusually thick skull. No damage, but the pain from the cut was blinding.

My parents were in the room waiting for me when I was wheeled back in. Looking at my mom I asked, "How's Chris?"

She smiled at me, Joyce says that he is doing fine. With the way you went down, you may find yourself here longer than him."

"Oh, ha-ha. I'm ready to get out of here," I said and then paused. "Do you think that they would let me go across the hall and see Chris?"

My dad looked up, "Maybe. I'll go ask at the nurse's station," and he strode out.

Mom sat down, "So truthfully, how do you feel?"

"Like I've been hit with a hammer; claw end first. How many stitches did they decide to use?

"According to the doctor, you only needed three. At least they are right at your hair line, so the scar won't be visible."

"Now there's a happy thought," I said sarcastically. My dad came back, and looking at him I raised my eyebrows.

"The nurse said that it was probably okay. She's getting you a set of wheels so that you can go visit." As he finished speaking, the Asian nurse from earlier came in pushing a wheel chair.

"Here you go," she said.

"I could've walked over."

"Hospital policy; either you are in a wheel chair on a gurney or a hospital staff member must accompany you until you are released."

"Joy."

"Yes?" she answered. "What is it?"

I stood dumbfounded then comprehension sunk in. I had said the word sarcastically, but that was her name. "Nothing. Sorry."

Getting wheeled over was not the highlight of my time here, but at least I was going to get to see Chris.

Entering into the room, I was shocked to see how full it currently was. As Joy pushed me through the small entrance hall, I counted two doctors, Joyce and Mark as well as once police officer that was trying to be inconspicuous. "Hope we're not intruding," Joy announced as she pushed me in.

"Stevie?" What the heck happened to you?" Chris asked from the bed.

I looked up and felt my throat tighten.

His face was covered with what had to be several bruises on top of each other. Blood still stained the lower part of his face and his lips were swollen to twice normal size. His left eye was swollen to the point that I doubted that he could see out of it. And he was worried about me.

"Oh, Chris. My God, what did they do to you? Jump you and perform the entire show of *Riverdance*?"

Chris's swollen lips curved in a smile, "Ouch! Have to remember that I can't do that. Hurts pretty bad." He sipped water through a straw.

As he tried to move, the sheet slipped off and I saw the rest of his body was covered with bruises as well. I propelled myself closer to Chris's bed while the doctors left with his parents. My parents followed, leaving us alone.

"Chris, really, what happened?"

He shrugged. "I'm not a hundred percent sure, actually. It appears that after Tony and a few of his friends heard the rumor from the Ditzy Duo, they decided that they needed to find out for themselves. Thanks for the text by the way. If I hadn't been expecting something I think this would have been a lot worse."

"I'm sorry. If I hadn't slipped yesterday, none of this would have happened."

"Hey, no feeling sorry for yourself in here. Positive thinking only." He nodded when I smiled.

His face went blank again. "I've been trying to think about what happened so I can tell the police. Normally for gym, I change in the Handicap shower stall in the back of the locker room. Since you had given me the warning, I took my stuff and went to the bathrooms in the front of the locker room and started to get changed. I figured it would be a little safer since they were closer to the office and potential help. Apparently Tony and pals saw me changing, and broke the stall door down."

Tears began to well up in his eyes. "When they pulled me out, I was only half dressed. So there I stood in my shorts, with my bindings wrapped around my breasts. They may have been bound, but they were still visible, as were the facts that I have a few other feminine attributes. That's when they started pounding on me. Ian came in only a few seconds later, but they had gotten in enough hits." He looked up at me with pain that did not come from a physical injury, "Everybody knows, Stevie. There is no hiding Chrissy now, they all know about her. Of course, my parents are supremely ticked; my mom is worried about me, while Mark is trying to figure out what we should do. My life is a wreck."

"Chris, we'll figure this out. You guys have been there for me; we'll all be there for you. There are only a few more months until graduation. You said you were planning to transition over the summer. Perhaps most of the hoopla will die down before then."

"Mark thinks I should do it now. He says that since everybody knows, I should show 'em what a girl I am."

"I'm not sure that would be good right now."

"I don't know. We're going to have to talk about it. Mom is setting up a meeting with the shrink. Of course, it's going to be a few days before I'm back anyway. I've got to wait for the bruises to fade, and I'd like to give the ribs a bit of time so they don't always hurt."

They came in to wheel Chris to a new room since he was going to be spending the night. Joy assured me that they would be in to finalize my release shortly. So as I waited alone in the little room, I thought again about how I needed to find a way to keep my friends safe.

Seeing Chris like that; bruised head to toe and devastated left me even more concerned. If whatever was pulling me into those weird dreams pulled him in now, there was a fair chance that he wouldn't make it back.

No, the only choice that I had was to pull back from everyone, and keep pushing at the clue by myself. That way any negative energy would be focused on me and only me.

By the time I got home that night, I was an emotional wreck. So far this week had been the-roller-coaster-ride-from-hell. Between the issues with Emily, nearly killing my brother, getting seduced by the Ditzy Duo, spilling my guts about my friends, throwing up at school, and everything that had happened to Chris, I was spent. I climbed the stairs to go to my room, shuffling my feet on the carpet in the hall. When I touched the knob to the door, ZAP!. I looked over at Misty who was sitting by my foot, "I hate static electricity." Unlatching the door, I was about to go in, when Kyle's door opened.

"Hey, Stevie. You got a minute?"

I'm not sure if it was guilt or something else that had me feeling sorry for the way he looked right now. "Yeah, what's up, Kyle?"

He looked flustered. "Is what they're saying about Chris true? I mean, does he really look like a girl?"

Ooh! Why me? "Yeah, I guess he does."

"Why?"

"Kyle, I'm not sure what to say. Chris confided in me, and I've already broken that confidence."

"Stevie, I know. I mean the rumor around school is that he's queer; he's trying to turn himself into a chic."

"Look, Kyle, Chris has a medical condition and has been in treatment for the past few years. Part of the treatment, is what caused the developments that everyone is now so concerned about."

"Okay. I guess that makes sense. Thanks." He retreated back into his room leaving me standing alone in the hall.

Closing my door, I curled up on my bed. I wanted to call someone that I could talk about everything with. But whom could I trust? I couldn't call Chris; he was too close to the situation. Emily? She was nearly as distraught as I was. I found out that after I collapsed, they had to sedate her. Ian might be a good answer, but I felt that I was already dumping too much on him. Keeping this secret for only a few days had been so hard. The realization that Chris had kept this from everyone for so long made me feel a new empathy for him. I could only hope that Mark would relent a bit, or Chris's senior year was going to have a very interesting end.

I closed my eyes and drifted into a very restless sleep filled with witches, and horsemen.

CHAPTER 19

COMING TO TERMS

I spent the next two days wishing that I could find a way to perfect time travel. I so wanted to find a way to avoid spilling the beans about Chris and causing this disaster that was currently plaguing me. Reality however, doesn't allow for that.

When the alarm went off in the morning, I haphazardly slapped the snooze button and let myself drift back to sleep. Apparently, I didn't hear it go off the next time, because when I woke, it was to the feel of ice-cold pellets that were touching me. "Hey! What the heck?" I exclaimed as I tried to roll away.

I became aware of my mom's laughter at my feeble attempts of escape. "Maybe next you'll remember to get up, sleepy head, before I have to resort to my collection of frozen ball bearings."

For as long as I can remember, Mom has always kept a small plastic container of steel ball bearings in the freezer. I always asked her why she kept them, and she'd say they were for the day that one of us wouldn't get out of bed. It took until today for me to get the picture.

No matter how I moved on my bed, those blasted frozen spheres rolled to wherever I touched the mattress, and voila, ice cold against my skin. The only escape was to get up. "Okay, okay, you win. I'm getting up." Once my feet hit the floor, I looked at my mom. There was definitely a sparkle in her eyes. "Well, I'm glad that I was able to amuse you so early this morning."

"You did. I have to admit, those things are quite effective."

"If I said that it wasn't nice, would it matter?"

"Nope. You slept through the alarm, me calling you and now you're running about thirty minutes late. You left me little choice."

"You win. Take your miniscule torture devices and go. I'll be down in a minute.

Deciding that I really didn't have time for a shower today, I simply pulled my hair into a ponytail and threw on a pair of sweats. Rushing downstairs, I grabbed a chocolate chip muffin and a diet coke on my way through to the back hall and my jacket.

Checking the clock, I discovered that I was only running about three minutes ahead of the bus, so I slipped on my Uggs and made a dash out the door.

The regular groups of students were already huddled around the actual stop. Emily was standing a bit of a ways down, but that wasn't unusual these days. Since the attack on Chris, the school hadn't been able to break any of the suspects. Ian and Chris had both named the same group of students, but they were sticking with their story. Unfortunately, as Sheriff Guliano had predicted, the lab work was taking longer than anticipated. They were making progress, but there was still going to be some time before any resolution.

Emily and I had never been among the "in" crowd, so we were used to being ignored. After the attack, however, many of the students blamed us for getting their friends in trouble. Like we were the ones that made them go and gang up on Chris. It was ludicrous.

Luck must have been working against me on every little thing this morning. Not only was I late getting up this morning, but the bus was late too. Not that I really minded, since it was one of those rare spring mornings: sunny and in the sixties.

The bus finally arrived fifteen minutes late, so it was obvious that we weren't gong to have much time once we got to the building before homeroom. "It's interesting," I said to Emily, "to see the number of kids who apparently didn't do their homework last night now scribbling something down so they can pretend to have made an effort."

Emily checked her watch. "It's going to be real close, us getting there on time today."

"Yeah.   Thankfully I have everything that I need for orchestra with me, so I'm just heading right for homeroom. I'll hit the locker after first."

"I'm thinking of doing the same. I've got the bare essentials with me. If I need something else, I'll get Sweeney to give me a pass out."

We paused as the bus pulled into the bus circle. "Look over there," someone from the back of the bus said loudly.

Everyone turned to look out the window towards the school. There were at least fifty kids gathered around in a semi circle. "What the heck?" I wondered.

Emily craned her neck, hoping for a better view. "It's hard to tell, but it looks like Lerch and another teacher just took someone in. This day is just getting more and more interesting."

As soon as the bus stopped, it was a mad dash for everyone to get off and into homeroom. Breathlessly, I ducked into Mrs. Vallente's room just as the bell rang. "Cutting it close there, Ms. Nixon," she said with a smile. "Don't get comfortable though, they want you in the main office right away."

I swallowed hard but could only manage a squeaky, "Okay."

Pushing the door to the office open I walked in. "Okay, what's going on now?" I asked the other students who were sitting by the door.

Emily looked up and shrugged. "I don't know. That's what Ian and I were just discussing."

"You look totally exhausted," Ian said, as he pulled me in for a hug and a quick kiss. "Missed you this morning."

"Bus was late," I said with another shrug. "And I've got this crazy deadline thing hanging over my head, nothing to lose any sleep over. Any idea what was going on over by the side door this morning?"

"No," he said. "I noticed the commotion over there, but I didn't have any urge to go over and get in the middle of that mess."

The door to Mrs. Lerch's office opened, and Mrs. Croft stepped out, saw us sitting there and turned back to the office occupants, "The rest of them are here."

Mrs. Lerch's voice sounded tired when she said, "Send them right in, Mrs. Croft."

We all headed towards the door, hoping that we were going to get some explanation to what was going on.

Entering the office, Mrs. Lerch motioned us to the chairs. A girl who looked to be about our age already sat in one of the chairs. Her red hair was cascading over her face, while she sat and sobbed. I looked over at Emily and Ian warily. "I'm not sure that I understand why we're here, Mrs. Lerch."

"I asked for you," the girl sobbed. She looked up for the first time.

"Oh. My. God. Chrissy?" I stuttered.

"Yeah," she replied weakly. "I decided that I've had enough. I needed to be me, the real me."

"Chris," Emily said, and then paused. "Do you really think that this is in your best interest?"

"Emily," Chris replied, "I've been living with this secret for over thirteen years. It's eaten away at me, bit by bit. The person that most of the school knows me as is nothing more that a mask that I put on to avoid getting the crap beat out of me. Over the past year, things have gotten harder to hide due to the medication. And you know what my home life's been like with Mark. He's been threatening to ship me out for the last week. Everybody here at the school knows about my, um, developments. So why hide? It hurts too much. If they're going to kill me because of who, and what, I am, then it will be the real me that they kill."

I walked over and pulled Chrissy to her feet, gave her a hug. "I don't know how much help I'll be, but I'll do what I can."

Emily and Ian followed and the four of us stood there in the middle of the office in one big group hug.

"I hate to break this party up," Mrs. Lerch said. "But to be honest, we have several things that we have to figure out."

"Like what?" Emily asked. "Chrissy is dressed appropriately, though her make-up needs to be touched up. What else is there to take care of?"

I could see by the expression on Mrs. Lerch's face that we had missed a bunch. "Let's start with the restroom issue. Where do we let Chris—sy go? Or how about changing for gym class?"

"Hadn't thought about that," Ian said. We looked at each other, and then sat down in the scattered chairs of the office.

Ideas were tossed around for more than forty minutes before Chrissy's mom came in. "Christine! What on Earth are you doing here?"

Chrissy spoke in a demure voice that was a bit on the husky end for a girl. "Mom, you know how I feel. You know what Dr. Thomas said, that I needed to do this. I guess I figured since everyone knew, that it would be easier if I was just me."

"Easier on who?" Joyce demanded. "Mark is going to hit the ceiling when he finds out about this. I'd convinced him that this wasn't in your best interest right now. You do know that right? I thought that we had agreed that you could start being Chrissy around the house on the weekends when we were home. Wasn't that enough?"

Chrissy looked devastated. "Mom, please try to understand. This isn't some whim that I've got; it's a medical condition. One for which the doctors have prescribed medications for. Medications that have changed my body in drastic and permanent ways. Changes, which once the kids at this school heard about, prompted me to be physically attacked. I can't change the way that they view me, or how they feel about me. But what I can do is to be me. To go out with my head held high and be the best that I can be. Perhaps this will give my contemporaries a lesson that doesn't come from a book."

Silence hung in the air as each of us in the room pondered what Chrissy's statement meant for us. Finally, Mrs. Lerch broke into our thoughts. "I can see both sides to this argument. Chrissy, we are all here because we are worried about your safety. I can understand what it is like to be repressed and held back from what you really want, or need, to do. I believe that it would be in all of our best interests if we spent some time right now working together to find a solution that satisfies all of our concerns. But, I warn all of you, in order to find that solution, it is going to require all of us to compromise. We are going to have to face things that we really would rather not. Am I understood?" She looked around the room; everyone was nodding their head. "Okay, why don't we go into the conference room here and lets get started on making this a success story?"

Looking around the table four hours later, everyone looked as if they had just finished a marathon. Mrs. Lerch had called in the school psychologist again as well as the superintendent Mr. Russell, so we could get the entire district on one page. It had taken most of the day, but between the eight of us, we had managed to draft a pretty good plan that should let Chrissy get through the rest of the year.

Chrissy was sitting across the table from me, and honestly, I don't think that I'd ever seen someone smile as wide and as bright as she was right now. I could only imagine what she must be feeling like right this minute; to know that you are going to face everybody and attract some stares, but for the first time they will be seeing the real you.

My mind stopped on that thought. How did Chrissy have the courage to be the real her, while I was still struggling to find the real me? And was the real me, somehow attached to finding the solution to the clue?

I'd gotten caught up in helping Chrissy today, which was a good thing that I needed to do for a friend. But it also meant that I would need to spend extra time making up the assignments that I missed by not being in classes today. If I continued to spend too much time away from the task that I had been charged with, I would never get a chance to find the real me.

As we left the school that day, it had become apparent that several of the other students had seen Chrissy this morning, hence the group that Emily and I had seen as we arrived. But to be honest, most of the school really didn't have a clue what was about to happen. Mrs. Lerch was going to be having an assembly the next morning where she was going to share some information that Dr. Thomas had graciously sent to us that afternoon. As a group, we hoped that with some education, people as a whole would be more open to what was going on with Chrissy.

Honestly, I had doubts that it was going to make an impact on enough people to make a huge difference, but I had to hope. I also had to be honest with myself; while Chrissy was my friend, it was a bit weird. I knew the reasoning behind everything, but it left me with many questions about the situation. All I could do right now was hope that these questions would be answered somehow over the next few days.

As I rode the bus home that afternoon, I thought about the clue that I had let sit untouched for most of the last week. Time was running out on me, and I was starting to feel the pressure of failure breathing down my neck. Maybe it was a selfish idea, but I decided on that ride, that I was going to worry more about solving this clue than how I was going to be able to help Chrissy in school over the next few days.

Striding into the kitchen for a snack, I spied Kyle sitting on one of the stools at the breakfast bar. He looked worried about something. Well, I was here anyway; I could probably afford to pay him a little attention. "What's up, Kyle? You look lost."

His head jolted up and he focused on me. "Oh, hey, Stevie. I guess I'm a little distracted. I, mean, I'd heard about Chris before and all, but did he really show up today at school wearing a blouse and skirt?"

"Yeah, she did. She looked very nice today; a bit scared but overall anxious."

"Anxious for what? Don't you think that everybody is going to go after him tomorrow?"

"First of all, according to the doctor that we had a conference call with today, while Chris is presenting as a girl, we address her as Chrissy and use the feminine pronouns. Secondly, a group of us, including Mrs. Lerch, Mr. Russell, Chrissy's mom and the school shrink worked to come up with a plan that should allow this to all happen with out much in the way of confrontations. So we are going to hope..." I knew that I had trailed off towards the end, but was banking on Kyle missing it.

Of course he didn't. "You're concerned about this as well, but there is something else that is bothering you. Why don't you sit down, have a brownie and spill."

He may spend most of his life as my obnoxious, prankster of a little brother, but he understands what people need. I pulled out a stool and snagged the last brownie from the plate. "I guess I'm just worried about everything that is going on. I mean, we did about as much as we can for Chrissy and her situation, but it doesn't relieve me of the fact that I've got to find a way to solve this clue real soon. It hit me today, there is less than four days left, and I really don't have a good handle on this one."

Chugging some milk to wash down the gooey brownie, I sighed. "At this point in the last clue, I at least knew what I was supposed to do. In fact, I'd already done what I thought was the actual task."

"It wasn't," he added while getting more brownies from the pan. "But I can understand what you must be thinking. But don't forget, you solved that one in the eleventh hour, so it's not over until the fat lady sings."

Putting my dishes in the dishwasher, I turned to look at him. "That may be true, but she's warming up. Thanks for trying to keep my head from getting too overwhelmed."

CHAPTER 20

ATTACKED

After having a sleepless night, again, I watched the sunrise wondering what today would have in store for me. After yesterday's events, I didn't think that there would be much that could make the day more dramatic. I was wrong.

As the bus pulled into the loop, I was met with the first sign that things were not going to be a stroll down easy street. The front lawn of the school was crowded with people. "Oh my," I whispered to Emily.

"Do you think that all of these people are here because of Chrissy?"

"I can't think of any other reason for people to be gathered on the front lawn, or for that matter, why there would be news vans from every station in New York parked over there."

"I'd really hoped that this would be over now, and you know we could get back to things like, I don't know, learning perhaps."

"It's a nice thought," I said, but in my mind I agreed with her.

Putting my coat in my locker, I overheard two girls walking by. "That's one of its friends," the one whispered to the other.

I tried to block the sound, but aside from covering my ears, I had no option other than just ignoring what everyone else was saying., I let out a long sigh just as Ian strolled up behind me.

"You doing okay, Stevie?" he asked.

"Oh, yeah, just ducky," I said as I stood and gave the two gossipers a quick glance.

"I've got a feeling its going to be a very interesting day. People are already talking. You've seen the circus outside, and the kids seem to have a fairly set opinion of what's going on."

"Ian, what are we going to do? I mean, we came up with a plan yesterday that was supposed to head this all off at the pass. But now we've got reporters outside, protesters marching and we haven't even had a chance to explain what is going on."

"I think that the best thing that we can do right now is to follow our plans, and keep our eyes and ears open. Hopefully, Lerch's assembly will take care of the worst of this. We need to be there for Chrissy if this all crashes and burns."

"You're right, I suppose. But still it feels like there should be something else we can do."

"Oh, I'm sure that we could spend all of our waking hours trying to solve this by working up good PR, but we all have other things to do."

I stopped dead in the hall. "Ian. I've only got three more days to figure out the clue. I can't keep getting pulled into other crises."

He took my hand, "Relax, Stevie. We'll figure it out."

The assembly had lasted nearly an hour, but it seemed that there were still questions that everyone else wanted answers to. I did my best to keep from getting cornered, but still being supportive. The result? I was trying to hide in plain sight during most of my classes. Unfortunately, it didn't seem to be working. By the time I was in Physics, I was inventing reasons to sit behind the lab desk on the floor. Ian kept down looking at me. Finally he crouched down next to me. "Stevie, what are you doing on the floor?"

"Everyone is looking at me. They keep whispering about what's going on, and it's making me very uncomfortable."

"Listen, they're talking about all of us for being friends with Chrissy. But, that's what friends do: they stand for each other in good and bad times. Right now, Chrissy really needs our support."

I thought about what he was saying. Returning to Ian's side at the lab table, I said, "I guess that makes sense. I just don't know if I've got the reserve left to get through this."

I went to study hall feeling a little better. It turned out that when I'd listened to a few of the kids that were close by in Physics, they were actually talking about how brave it was for Chrissy to do what she was doing. That made a difference in how I was looking at things.

At my desk, I pulled out the notebook that I had been using for this clue. I knew that I really needed to get moving on this. I opened the pages and looked at the symbol that I'd copied over, along with the sketches from the medal.

I stared at it for a moment. The last clue had been given to me in Latin. Perhaps this was in a different language as well and I just needed to figure out which one.

I tried several different languages using my phone, but was coming up with nothing useful. I kept telling myself that a no was still an answer. Suddenly there it was! I looked again at what I thought were hieroglyphics. Sure enough, some of the symbols matched the ones on my phone; not hieroglyphics, but Greek!

I quickly scrolled through the Greek letters that were in the translation program. One by one, I was able to translate each letter. In the notebook I wrote:

Λοψαλιτιετ = **Loyalitiet**

I looked at what I'd written. I still didn't know what it meant, but at least it looked more comprehensible. Maybe a dictionary would help.

When the bell rang, I felt terrific. Progress had been made. I had something that I hadn't had when I'd walked in this morning. Now all I had to do was figure out what it actually meant.

Stepping into the hall, I immediately heard shouts and saw a group gathering around. From the number of teachers who were racing to the scene and the yells coming from there, I could only guess that there was a fight going on. I walked slowly towards the commotion; not because I'm one who wants to see people bloody each other, but it was the quickest way to my locker and French.

I could see the two people involved as I walked closer. I recognized the tall Amazonian build of Stephanie Elsmore as she delivered another crashing blow to her much smaller opponent. The crowd cheered when the small figure spun and fell to the floor in a swirl of blue and pink hair.

"Blue and pink hair?" I asked myself just as the realization hit. "Emily!"

Pushing my way into the crowd, I tried to get to Emily and was elbowed by several people. Emily, who was obviously afraid, was cowering and trying to protect her head. I saw Mr.

Zuhelgger and Mr. Crowe pulling Stephanie away from Emily. "Okay people, clear the halls," Mr. Crowe said as he waved people out of his way.

I reached Emily at about the same time as Mrs. Murphy came running down the hall. I cradled her, "Oh, Em, what happened?"

She looked up at me through an already swollen eye. "Got jumped. I guess people didn't like me sticking up for Chrissy, trying to get them to understand."

Mrs. Murphy arrived at this point. "Where did you get hit, dear, besides the obvious?"

"She hit me in the stomach several times," Emily winced as she moved. "She got a few shots into my face, but she seemed to concentrate on hitting me in the torso."

"Can you walk to my office, or do I need to send someone for the wheel chair?"

"I'll walk, if it's all the same to you."

I helped Emily get to her feet. "You want me to come with you, Em?"

Before Emily could answer, Mrs. Murphy did. "I think it would be best if you'd go to class. I'll take good care of her for now."

I nodded, and waited until they had turned the corner before I made my way to class. This was getting out of control.

Hiding in plain sight doesn't exactly work when you arrive to class late. "Sorry, Madame Lynn. There was a fight in the halls."

"So I've heard. Is Emily coming today?"

"I don't think so. She was one of the ones in the fight. She's with Mrs. Murphy right now."

"Ah, I see. Well, then, let's get started."

I made my way to my seat trying not to make eye contact with anyone. But I could feel the stares that focused on my back. I wondered if there was a plan amongst them to attack Chrissy and her friends individually, or if the attack on Emily was just some kind of fluke. Either way, it was a long class and my walk to lunch left me feeling quite anxious.

Setting my tray down at the table, I did something that I normally didn't do at lunch: I pulled out my iPod and shoved the earphones into my ears. Right now, I needed to escape reality for a few minutes and be alone in my own little world.

I closed my eyes and listened to the recorded voice coming through my ears and focused on making my toes relax. It took a full ten minutes for me to finally relax enough that I was willing to come back and try to eat my salad.

Opening my eyes, I first saw Ian sitting across from me eating his sandwich. He was leaned back in his chair, arms crossed over his chest and staring at me. "Welcome back," he said with a grin.

"Hi. Sorry. I needed to veg out for a few minutes."

"What were you listening to? Normally when you listen to music, you tap your foot and bounce. This time you were almost as still as a statue."

"I was listening to a recording of a relaxation technique."

"Guess the fight today got you a bit, eh?"

I shrugged, "I think it's more than just that, but it definitely adds to it. I'm down to having a few days left before the equinox." I paused as Chrissy came in wearing a modest blouse and skirt combo. I had to admit, that while it was a little strange seeing her here, she was doing a good job at trying to fit in and make the best of it.

"I almost forgot," I said, "I think I may have made a bit of progress on the clue."

"That's wonderful!" Chrissy said as she sat down and started to eat.

"What did you find?" Ian asked, sitting up straight now.

Between mouthfuls of salad and soup, I showed Ian my notebook. He had a strange look on his face. "What's up?" I finally asked.

"I think you're getting really close here. I was thinking about the symbols that we had found earlier at the library. Didn't the dog represent loyalty or something like that?"

I paused, "Yeah, I think so. Why?"

"Take a look at the root of this word. Kind of looks like loyal to me."

"Yeah, but that would almost be too easy."

I glanced up and noticed that several people around us were looking at us. At first, I thought that they were looking at Chrissy, but I realized that they were looking at all of us. "Um, I think we may have a problem here," I whispered to Ian, as Tony Despenzo came towards us.

"Yes, Tony?" Ian asked pleasantly. "Is there something that we can help you with?"

Tony stared at us. "This ain't right. You two are just as bad for hanging out with freaks. We already got one, its only gonna be a matter of time before we take care of you, too." He made a rude gesture with his hand.

"Thanks, Tony. You're number one in our book also," Ian said.

Tony grimaced, pointed his finger at the ceiling, and spun his hand in a circle. The others that had taken position around us retreated.

"Sorry about that guys," Chrissy muttered. "I thought that the goons would only go after me. I never imagined that they would give anyone else a hard time with this."

"It is what it is."

"Chrissy," I started, and then hesitated. "Don't you think that this would be better if you let it wait until after graduation?"

Chrissy sat in silence for a minute. "No. I needed to do this now. I couldn't wait."

"Stevie," Ian broke into the conversation. "This is a medical deal. Would you ask someone who is suffering to hold off on medical treatment until it was more convenient for you?"

"Ian, they're attacking us! Don't you get it?" I got up and bolted from the table.

Slamming my locker closed, I was still grumbling under my breath as I made my way towards English.

"Ah, isn't that a shame?" Gabby asked a laughing Tanya. "She looks upset. I wonder why?"

"Maybe it's because that guy in the skirt looks better than she does!" Tanya said with a laugh.

"Probably. What's wrong little Stevie? Did my cousin finally wake up and dump your butt? I would've."

I tried to walk by, but Tanya gave me a shove into the locker bank. "Hey, Stupid, watch where you're going. People who hang out with queers don't deserve to walk anywhere near me. Now be gone!"

They laughed as they walked away. I slid down the lockers, folding in on myself and just got more furious with myself.

By the time I'd calmed down, I was late for class. "Ms. Nixon that will be five minutes after school for being late. Next time, bring a pass."

"But Ms. Daily," I protested, "there were extenuating circumstances!"

"I'm sure that they seemed that way then, but this is now. Five minutes."

I trudged to my desk. "Nice job, Nixon," someone stage whispered. Another voice questioned, "Yeah, maybe her boyfriend needed a make-up lesson."

I dropped my books onto the desk and slumped in the chair. I had a little over ninety minutes left today.

Hearing the last bell of the day, my heart raced. I needed freedom from this place, from the bullies that had been having a good laugh at my expense today. I threw my books into my locker, and just headed out of the building. I didn't even pause to grab my jacket or purse. I wanted out.

Once clear of the building, I angled myself towards the woods and kept running. I needed the space from here. I felt the phone in my pocket vibrate, but I didn't take the time to look at it.

I tore into the woods, and stopped at the rock. This rock had starred in many of my dreams recently, and had been instrumental in the first stage of the quest.

In my dreams, this is where the evil witch is waiting for me. But now it seemed calm, no fire burning or nut job chanting. Just the sun streaming down into the open circle. I lay back on the rock, my face squinting in the sunlight and tried to empty my mind.

Whatever the next few days brought, I had to be ready. Right now, however, I was confused and upset. Not exactly the two adjectives that I wanted to use to describe my stated of mind.

I closed my eyes tightly, and began to do the relaxation exercises from the program that I had listened to earlier. As I felt my mind finally free itself from the torment that I had felt all day long, other ideas flowed in.

Loyaliteit, a dog, a flower and me. What was the connection?

CHAPTER 21

RETREAT

I woke in the morning with the feeling that a black cloud was hanging over me, just waiting until it could strike me down. I curled back into the covers and pulled the pillow over my head. In honesty, I dreaded the thought of getting out of bed and trying to make it through the day today.

By the time that I had gotten myself calmed down and pulled together yesterday, I had missed dinner and everyone here was having a panic attacks. I skipped eating all together opting instead to just go to my room and have some quiet time.

No one had seemed to make too big of a deal of it last night, but I knew that I was going to have to talk to someone sooner or later today. I was planning to choose latter, much latter.

When I was still awake twenty minutes later, I forced myself to crawl out of my warm bed and put on a face that gave the impression of being happy. I glanced at my desk calendar as I made my way to the closet. I knew what today was, and the reminder that the equinox was in just two days was enough to make me begin to hyperventilate.

The cold stark reality was that I didn't have much time left.

I tried to push the thought from my mind and continued on to my closet to select an outfit for the day. Unfortunately, my mind wouldn't let go of this. I wasn't ready to go yet; I still had too many things that I wanted to do in this life before I checked out.

I also found myself getting worked up, thinking about school today. Yesterday had been a fiasco; I'd been verbally bullied several times, Emily had been hit so hard that she'd ended up with a concussion. The part that really got to me about Emily's situation was that she'd never even tried to defend herself, but she still ended up getting a three-day suspension for fighting.

Things were just not going well right now. Pulling on my sweater, I wondered what my Mom would say about just skipping school today.

I was just starting to work over how I would approach it with her when I heard the knock on the door.

Misty came running in and jumped onto my lap and covered my face with doggie kisses. "Yes. Yes, you are a good dog!" I said rubbing her back and watching her little stub of a tail wag so fast it almost blurred.

I heard the floorboard creak, and turned towards the door. "Mom."

"I was hoping that we could talk, Stevie." When I nodded, she sat on the edge of the bed. "I'm getting a bit worried about you, Honey. You didn't call last night, came in late and then hid in your room all night.

I thought for a very brief moment. This was my mom; I'd never kept secrets from her before this whole curse thing had started. "Mom, there has just been so much going on. I mean, you know about the clue, and I only have two more days on that."

I took a deep breath before I continued, "Then, there is everything that is going on with Chrissy. Dealing with that at school has been boatloads of fun. Never knowing if the person who is coming up behind you wants to congratulate you or punch you. It's got my nerves on end. Topping it all off, I'm worried about Emily."

"What happened with Emily?"

"Oh, I thought Kyle would have told you last night. Stephanie Elsmore jumped her and beat her pretty seriously yesterday in the hall. She ended up going to the hospital with a concussion."

"Why did Stephanie do that? She was always a nice girl, big for her size, but sweet and all."

"Well, yesterday, she put all of her big into hurting Emily. Best guess that anyone has is because Emily was standing up for Chrissy, trying to help things there. The situation doesn't exactly sit well with everyone."

"I guess I can see that. But remember, Chrissy is the same person she was before you knew everything. Now she's just showing her true self."

"I keep trying to remember that, but it's been hard dealing with that and the clue at the same time."

"I know you'll figure out how to make it work, Stevie." She pulled me in and gave me a hug. "Now, why don't you get ready for school, and I'll make some chocolate chip pancakes. Okay?"

"I guess if I've gotta go."

"Yes, you've got to. Now get ready." She left me there thinking about what my future held in store.

Hoping that something would come up and get me out of having to face things at school, I finished packing my book bag and headed downstairs. I kept trying to figure out what I was going to do about the clue, but continued to come up empty.

Kyle was already downstairs when I got there. "Hey, Kyle," I prompted while I poured orange juice.

"Is it true what I heard last night? That the Elsmore girl pounded on Emily?"

I nodded. "Yeah. I was there at the end of the fight, and found Em on the floor. Thankfully the teachers got everyone out of the way before it got any worse."

"That had to be brutal. I mean, Stephanie has at least six inches and probably fifty pounds on Emily. Is she okay?"

"That depends on your definition of okay. She ended up with a concussion, and got suspended for three days. She should recover, but they said that there may be some permanent damage to her one eye."

"Sheesh. Why can't people just let everyone go their own way?" He bit into his stack of pancakes and looked thoughtful. "Stevie, do me a favor. Watch your back. I know that you've been friends with Chris for almost forever, but with what's going on right now, you may want to back off a little. Keep a little extra distance until this all blows over."

Part of me hated that idea, but I had to admit, there was a part of me that had already thought about doing that. It wouldn't take too much to think up some excuse why I couldn't meet up with Chrissy for a few days. It would give me a little space and time to solve the clue and take care of this step of the quest. "Yeah," I sighed, "I think that might be a good idea as well."

We didn't say much through the rest of breakfast. It was lonely riding the bus by myself, knowing that my best friend was home recovering. I closed my eyes and let myself hope that today would be better than yesterday.

School turned out to be a repeat of yesterday, only this time I wasn't able to avoid all of the comments. The bullying picked up right where it had ended yesterday. I ended up going to Mrs. Lerch to complain about what was going on.

"We're working on it, Stevie. Please, just try to be patient. I know that there have been many issues, but we are trying to put out as many of the fires as we can," she said while I was in her office. She held up a stack of messages, "These are the calls, just from today, that I have to respond to. Parents, the media and every other person who has some form of opinion on this."

"I understand, Mrs. Lerch. I do. But isn't there anyway that we can convince people to let this go? I feel like I'm just waiting for the pummeling to begin every time I'm in the hall. Somebody is going to really get hurt if we don't put an end to this soon."

"I've left word with Sheriff Guliano. I'm hoping that we can put something together within the next few hours to help settle this down. I really thought that by having the assembly with the doctors and all there, that this would be non-issue."

"I think," I hesitated, "that for many it is a non-issue. But it only takes a few to incite a riot."

Ignoring the stares and the whispers, I pushed through the rest of the day. I guess the up side of the day was nobody tried to stab me in the back; everybody said what they felt to my face. I didn't think that I could feel much worse than I did yesterday afternoon, but I was wrong.

By the time that the bell rang for the end of the day, I was finding excuses to hide from everybody, including Ian and Chrissy. I figured that the less I was seen with Chrissy right now, the easier people would be on me. In a way it was kind of like that old saying about meeting a bear in the woods. I didn't have to outrun the bear; only the person I was with. In this case, all I had to do was be out of the way of the mob, and theoretically I'd be left alone.

I quickly got what I needed out of my locker and then headed down the back stairs. I ducked into the locker rooms to wait until everyone had left the building. Curling up on one of the wooden benches, I pulled out my notebook and kept staring at my handwritten notes, hoping that something would jump off of the page and give me the inspiration to solve the clue. Unfortunately, I didn't see anything new.

I needed to spend some time going over what we had put together over the past three months, but the bench wasn't that comfortable, and I could hear the sounds of the basketball team in the halls. It was time for me to find a different perch for my thinking.

I went out the back door of the building. The lot, as I'd hoped, was pretty much empty, so I felt fairly safe in walking around. I knew that I had almost two hours before the late buses would be ready, so I needed a place to go that would give me physical and mental comfort. I looked across the street and saw the answer.

Jogging across the street, I opened the door to Scoops, and stepped in. I was about to give the waitress a casual wave when I noticed two people sitting at the booth near the back wall. Gabby and Tanya were watching me with interest. Glancing the other direction, I noticed that several other students were now watching intently. I turned to make my way out and stopped dead in my tracks. Chrissy was sitting at a table with someone I didn't know, watching me.

I swallowed hard and walked over. "Hi Chrissy," I said trying to sound cheerful.

"Pull up a seat," she said patting the chair next to her.

"I really don't have time today, I thought I'd, um get something to go." I turned and headed out hastily. Muttering under my breath, "Why is it my luck that the one person I was hoping to avoid would be sitting right there?" I ignored the pedestrians on the street who kept glancing at the strange girl talking to herself.

I felt a tug on my sleeve and spun around.

"Chrissy! You scared me."

"Stevie, I've known you for how long? What's eating you?"

Shuffling my feet, I closed my eyes and wondered why nobody was striking me dead right now. How could I tell someone who has been one of my closest friends for a decade that I needed some time away right now? "Chrissy, we've shared a lot of things over the years. But right now, I'm really freaking out."

"Is it me?" she asked. I could tell by the tone in her voice that I'd hurt her more than I ever wanted to.

"Oh, Chrissy," I gave her a hug. "You know that I still love you as a friend. And I'm going to support you as best as I can. But right now, I'm down to two days until the equinox. And I don't have the time to deal with things right now."

She snapped like I'd slapped her. I could see the tears in her eyes as she fled.

"Great work, Stevie," I said to myself. "You've alienated everybody."

I turned and walked not in the direction of the school, but towards the cemetery.

I wandered aimlessly through the headstones that were filled with Sleepy Hollow's history. Some of these stones dated back to the early seventeen hundreds. I let my hand rub over the faded limestone, occasionally stopping to look at the names that had been engraved by the family of the deceased.

I kept weaving between the rows noticing the names; often several matching last names were grouped together. Looking up, I saw a single stone, atop the small hill flanked by a cherry tree that was just beginning to blossom. But it wasn't the tree that caught my attention. It was the carving of a dog carrying a flower that graced the top of the stone.

I walked over to the faded stone, rubbed my hand over it. "Ichabod Crane," I read. "Figures." I looked at the rest of the stone, hoping that there would be some miraculous find here that would tell me what the clue was. There was nothing that I could find that was going to help me.

I continued wandering, and I came across a series of stones embossed 'Von Brunt', my kin. An idea struck: what nationality was Von Brunt and Crane? The picture on Crane's stone matched the one on the medal. Maybe that would tell me what language I needed to use to solve my clue.

I turned and ran towards the exit. Time was running out, and besides, I was dying to get out of here.

CHAPTER 22

ALL ALONE

Getting home, I rushed into the kitchen. "Mom!"

"What is it, Stevie? Was there an accident?" she asked as she emerged from the kitchen drying her hands on a dishtowel.

"No," I gasped out of breath. "I had a thought that might help with the clue. What nationality are we descended from?"

She stared at me blankly. "I can't say as though I know offhand. We can give your grandparents a call. Perhaps they would know."

So, that's what I did. Of course, the way that my luck was running today, they had picked tonight to go out so I had to settle with leaving them a message. I hoped that they would get it early enough for me to make use of the knowledge before it got too late.

Knowing that I needed to find a way to get my mind off of everything, I changed my clothes grabbed a snack and headed out to my shop. Flipping on the lights, I stood in the doorway and admired the gleaming fuselage that only months before had been several flat sheets of aluminum. I walked around it, running my hand over the edges and convincing myself that I would be around to see it take to the air one day.

Working with the plans and shaping the metal always took me away from my day-to-day problems. I was counting on that. I switched on the radio to a top-forty station and let the music and the task at hand take over my mind. It didn't take long before I was so totally immersed in the project, and didn't even hear the radio any longer.

I had discovered that building a plane was at first glance a very daunting task. But when it really came down to it, it was nothing more than a series of relatively small, simple steps that were taken in a sequential order. Sometimes, however, those steps were enough to drive you crazy. Today's job was to run the wires from the instrument panel to the electrical bus.

Now, my Sonex wasn't going to have a ton of equipment on it. A simple radio, GPS and a basic set of instruments, and that's it. So here I sat, trying to figure out why I was dealing with nearly a hundred small wires. I finally decided that the best thing to do was to make up a series of wires that were all going to the same place instead of trying to run each wire individually.

Of course, I realized now that in order for me to get these wires into the area behind the panel, I would have to lay with my back on the floor and my feet over the seats and contort myself to reach each device. As I was lying there trying to snake my arm up between the fuel line and the bulkhead, I was wondering why I didn't make the panel so that it could be taken out with a few screws, and thankful that there wasn't anybody here to see me in this ridiculous position.

Soft footsteps echoed in the main part of the shop. "Hello?" I called. "Is somebody there?"

"Hey, Stevie, I just wanted to talk for a bit. Your mom said you were out here."

"I'll be up in a second, Ian," I said as I tried to contort myself in a way that would let me gain enough leverage to get up. With much grunting and straining, I finally emerged from the fuselage.

Ian was watching me with raised eyebrows, but I could tell that there was something on his mind. "What's up?" I asked tentatively as I walked to the small fridge that I kept out here full of soft drinks.

"Stevie," he began. He was wringing his hands, which signaled that this was not going to be good. He stammered, looked up at the ceiling and pinched the bridge of his nose. "I don't know where to begin exactly."

I handed him a Coke, and leaned back on the worktable with my own. "Is there something that I did that had you upset, Ian?"

"You could say that. I got a phone call from a very upset Chrissy. I thought that you were her friend. What happened?"

Oh boy, I thought. "Ian, I'm not sure what Chrissy said, but I'm trying to be there for her. But right now, I don't have the time for the dramatics."

"Chrissy called me, in tears. She said that you both had words downtown, and now she feels like you're abandoning her. All she's asking for is for you to stand with her and watch her back."

"Watch her back!" I yelled. "Emily is recovering from a concussion and has a three day suspension because she stood up openly for Chrissy. What's happening right now sucks! I've got a friend who wants me to be there to help, but it puts me in harms way. I've got a bloody witch who is causing me all sorts of grief, and a clue that I can't find a solution to. To top the whole pile off, if I don't manage to get everything together, I'm toast!" I threw my hands in the air, knocking my Coke off of the table. I looked up to the ceiling, hoping that I would find the right words to say. "Ian, all of these things are important. And each one is more important than the others to specific people. But right now,

I've got to do what is right for me. I've got to find the solution to the clue."

"Stevie, nobody is asking you to forgo working on things. All I'm saying is that you can't forget your friends. When you needed help with the first clue, who was there working with you? Emily, Chris and me. We stood by, helping with whatever we could, helping to make you successful. That's all Chrissy is asking for right now. She needs her friends to stand with her as she faces what has to be one of the toughest events in her life. She deserves your support."

"My support? She has that. She's had that for quite a while. I've done what I could to help her after I found out about what she was going through. I've been there to pick her up after she's had a round with Mark or her mom. Heck, I was there the other day when she came to school for the first time, and helped put the plan together for her. But right now, Ian, right now I've got less than two days to solve my problem. If I don't have a solution, I'm done! They'll be planting me down in the old cemetery near my relatives who have died over the last two-hundred years."

"Enough!" Ian bellowed. He stood there with a scowl on his face and his arms crossed over his chest. "This time, Stevie, I think that you have really overstepped your bounds. No one gave you grief about the curse that had been placed on your family! No one! Yet, here you are throwing it all back in our faces that your problem is more important than anyone else's! It's ludicrous. You're an incredibly sweet girl, who is very smart. But you tend to be selfish at times. And this is one of those times. You've got a friend who really needs help. Now! Not in two days. You may not want to think about it like this, but there is still time to work through the clue. Chrissy is having issues right this minute!"

"Ian," I fought to keep my voice reasonable. I had been the first to yell, but the truth of the matter was that if one of us didn't find a way to back off a bit, we were going to have fireworks here in the shop. "Right now I can't help her! Heck, I'm not sure that I can even help me right now." I began to pace around the work area. "I'm not sure that you fully understand the pressure that I'm under right now. My whole family knows about this curse, and I have to watch each one grow wary as the dates draw nearer. I'm so worried right now that I don't know what to do. That's part of the reason that I came out here tonight. I needed to have some time to find me. To calm myself down to a point that allows me to think straight."

"Well, you'd better figure things out pretty quick. We've been trying to give you the help that you needed along the way, but at this point someone else needs us. And if you're so blasted pig-headed as to be able to ignore your friends, then there isn't much that I can do for you. It doesn't matter how much I love you, or feel that you make my life better, if you can't do the right things at the right time, I don't think that I want to be with you."

"Ian, what are you talking about?" I turned on him.

"What I'm saying, Stevie, is that right now one of your best friends really needs you, and you're ignoring her. I don't want to spend time with someone who only cares about herself. So, right now it looks like you've got a choice to make. Are we going over to Chrissy's or what?"

"Ian!" I wailed, "I can't right now. I've got too much going on here trying to finish up the clue. Don't you get it?"

"Yeah, I do. I'll see you around." He turned and walked to the door of the shop. He stopped and looked back at me. "Everyone has choices to make. How we're going to spend our time, whom we'll spend it with and what we want to do with our lives. You've made your choice, Stevie. I hope that you won't regret it later." He closed the door behind him and I listened, as the footsteps grew fainter.

I rushed to the door, wrenched it open and called, "Ian!" He never turned around; he simply got into his car and pulled away.

Tears ran hot down my cheeks as I folded into a fetal position and fell against the wall. "How could I be so stupid?" I asked the few stars that were visible. At that moment, I felt like I'd lost everything. The person who had kept me centered for the past six months had just walked out of my life with less than a backwards glance. Who knew if he, or any of my other friends, would ever talk to me again?

"Why is life so unfair?" I sobbed into the still March night. I laid my head on my crossed arms and tried to come to terms with everything. Was I that wrong? Was trying to take care of the bigger picture less important than dealing with someone who had their feelings hurt? I didn't have the answers and each question that I thought of just kept emphasizing how insignificant it was.

I sat there on the floor, weeping and thinking. I felt a blanket being draped over me, and the soothing voice of my mom finally broke through. "It's okay, Stevie. Your first break-up is never easy, especially if you're the one being dumped."

"I screwed up, Mom. It's that simple. I. Screwed. Up," I said emphasizing each word.

"Now, Honey, it may seem like that right now, but it almost always takes two to make, or break, a relationship. Do you want to tell me what happened?"

I shrugged. "I'm not really sure what happened. Ian came over because Chrissy called him. Ian was upset with me because he feels that I'm not giving Chrissy the support that she needs. I tried to reason with him that right now I'm so tied up with trying to make it through this curse, that I don't have the time to waste with the drama of what is going on."

"Oh, Stevie," she said in a very sympathetic tone. "Right now your friend is going through a very rough time. She needs your help to stay strong. What happened today between you, anyway?"

I relayed how I'd gone into Scoops, tried to get out and then the conversation with Chrissy that had followed. "I'm trying to be there for her, but right now, I've got so much on my plate and I'm starting to get petrified about the possibility that I may not make this one."

"Maybe you spent too much time in the cemetery," she said trying to make me smile. It almost worked.

"No, really, Stevie. You can't get yourself all worked up about this curse business. And before you say anything, yes it is easy for me to say, because I'm not the one that is on the block. But you are. It's my daughter that we are talking about. Do I want to lose you? No way! But I also know that I have a job to do and responsibilities that I need to take care of as well as helping you. I can't ignore Kyle just because the deadline is looming so large in front of you. Believe it or not, you can stretch your time, and do all of these things." She leaned in and kissed my forehead. "I'm going to go back in now. So why don't you think about what it is that you want to do, okay?"

"Okay, Mom. Thanks for being here tonight."

"That's what I'm here for." She took a few steps and then turned back. "Stevie, be sure to think about how you'd like people to work with you if you were in their situation." With that, she strolled back to the house leaving me in my own thoughts.

Silence again embraced me. I leaned back and closed my eyes and thought about our conversation. I thought about the other definitive moments in my life, when I'd really needed her for something, and no matter what she was doing, she'd put it aside and come out to help me.

Thinking back to those times, I was pretty sure that there would have been cases where she'd had an important deadline, but she never once put me off. Her words began to resonate with me. I was using the crutch of what I was trying to overcome as an excuse to get out of doing something that was beyond where I wanted to be.

Chrissy had been dealing with this problem for so long, and was just now finding the strength to stand up and take those tentative steps, but she needed someone's hand to hold. And I'd pulled mine back when she'd reached for it.

I pulled out my phone, and was just about to call Chrissy, when it rang in my hand. I didn't recognize the number. "Hello?" I answered cautiously.

"Hey, Kiddo,"

"Poppy! Where are you guys? I didn't recognize the number."

"Oh we've been over visiting a neighbor, playing some bridge. Your grandmother decided that she should check the messages, and let me know that you called. So, what can I do for you?"

"I had a thought this afternoon. I ended up walking through the cemetery and noticed that there were several graves there that had the Von Brunt name on them. I also found one that was marked Ichabod Crane. Crane's headstone had the same dog carrying a flower on it that is on the medal."

"Is that so? Hmmm. That's kind of weird, don't you think?"

"Yeah, but I actually found it more interesting and intriguing when I put it together with what we thought were the hieroglyphics. I think that they are actually Greek letters. But when I translated the letters, I ended up with a word that doesn't make any sense."

"Okay, that's a lot to sift through right now, but it sounds like you've made some progress."

"Yep. I've definitely made some progress today, which brings me to what I called about. I'm wondering what nationality Von Brunt was?"

"That's an interesting segue. I think, though I can't swear to it, but I'm pretty sure that he was of Dutch decent. Why?"

"I'm thinking that the word that I ended up with after changing the Greek letters, is a word in the language of the people of the time."

"That seems like a stretch, but it does give you something to try. Anything else?"

"Nope. That's it. Thanks Poppy for being there for me."

"No problem. Glad to help my favorite grand-daughter."

"Poppy, I'm you're only grand-daughter."

"Oh, yeah? Well you're my favorite anyways. Take care, Kiddo."

I sat there thinking about what to do next. I looked at my phone and scrolled through until I found the number that I wanted. Unfortunately it went right to voice mail. "Hey, Chrissy. I wanted to apologize for how I acted today. I've been stressing about the deadline, and I've been acting like a jerk. I hope that you can forgive me. Well take care, and I'll see you tomorrow in school. Call me later if you want to talk. Bye now."

I stared at the phone in my hand. I couldn't dwell on the mistakes that I'd made but I had tried to correct them. Right now, however, I needed to go in and see if putting a Dutch spin on the clue helped.

CHAPTER 23

TURN OF THE TIDE

Racing into the house, I slammed the door and ran up to my room for my computer. I was amazed at the realization that whenever you are in a hurry, the computer seems to take three times longer to load. Today was no exception. For some odd reason, my computer didn't want to connect to the wireless router that my dad had installed. As each second ticked by, my frustration level increased exponentially.

When I finally managed to get logged on, it only took a few minutes for me to load up a free language translator. I typed in the word from my notebook, set the computer to translate from Dutch to English and hit the go button on screen. It only took seconds before the word popped up on screen. Loyalitiet translated to loyalty.

I leaned back and closed my eyes and sighed a heaven sent thanks. I finally had figured out what the clue was; now I just had to figure out to whom, where or what I was supposed to show my loyalty.

"Mom! Dad!" I called out. "I've got it! I figured out the clue!"

I heard the commotion from down stairs as they hurried up to my room. "What's up, Stevie?" my dad asked as he came through the door.

I pointed to the computer screen, "I did it! I solved the clue."

Mom came into the room, while Kyle leaned in the doorframe. "That's wonderful, Honey," Mom said as she hugged me.

"So what does it mean?" Kyle asked.

I told the story of how I'd figured out the Greek letters and how I'd come up with the thought while I was in the cemetery. "When Poppy called, he said that he thought the Von Brunt name came from the Dutch. So I took the word that I'd found at school and translated it from Dutch to English. It all fits now. The dog and the flower were both symbols of loyalty when used on coats of arms in the seventeenth and eighteenth centuries." I was smiling ear to ear. For the first time in over a month, I actually felt like I was going to be able to conquer this particular clue and challenge.

"Hmmm," Dad said, "so what happens next?"

My smile faded. "I don't know. Now I've got to try a figure out something that I am supposed to be loyal to." The reality hit: I had taken nearly three months to translate the clue, but now I only had a little less than forty-eight hours to complete whatever action I needed to. The problem was that right now, I had no idea what it was I was supposed to do.

Tossing and turning that night didn't help me sleep any better than I had for the last few weeks. The best that I had been able to manage by three-eighteen was a fitful nap that had lasted for all of about twenty minutes. I was having problems turning off my mind; the thought of not knowing what I was supposed to do now was extremely disturbing.

I headed towards the bathroom with every intention of taking some kind of sleeping pill. Normally, I hated doing this, but right now I knew that I needed the sleep so I was willing to take the desperate measures.

I was doing so well, or so I thought. I made it to the bathroom doorway, and put my hand out to feel for the light switch when my brother's door flew open and Kyle was standing there with a flashlight aimed at my chest.

"Yessh!" I squeaked, clutching my chest. "Why don't you scare me to death?"

"I was going to say the same to you. Why are you sneaking around at this time of morning?"

"Couldn't sleep. What are you doing up right now?"

"Heard someone creeping around in the hall."

I shook my head. "Go to bed, Kyle."

"Sorry about the heart-attack and all. Night." Once his door closed, I finished my mission to the medicine cabinet.

Apparently, we didn't have any actual sleeping pills, but I found some Tylenol PM. Cupping my hand to catch some water, I popped two and hoped for the best.

Floating through the mist, I felt myself flying again. I heard the all-too-familiar cackle of the witch at the clearing, and the distant sounds of some unseen horseman. The clearing came into view, and suddenly I was in the clearing opposite the witch.

"You've made more progress than ye were meant. But now your time is nearly spent. Ye have the word, ye got the clue. But ye shan't figure what to do. Let it go, accept the dark, take upon ye my eternal mark," she crooned as she stirred the cauldron suspended over the fire.

"You haven't won yet, you old witch! I'm never going to give in to you," I yelled.

Her eyes trained on me, and for the first time, I noticed that they were blood red. A wicked grin spread upon her face. "Then return to whence ye came, let us finish this deadly game. Where kin and friends lay this will end today. When ye have lost, it's for eternity ye shall pay the cost." Her hand shot out towards the cauldron, and there was a flash of light.

I sat upright with a gasp. I was in my room, in my own bed. Sun was beginning to stream in through the window, and I felt exhausted. I looked at the clock on the nightstand, "Ten-thirty! Oh no."

Jumping from the bed, I dropped my night clothes were I stood. The fact that they were drenched only barely made its way into my consciousness. Reaching into my closet, I grabbed the first pair of jeans I found and a sweater from the shelf. I was forcing my feet into my sneakers when there was a knock on the door.

"Stevie? Are you up, Honey?"

"Mom, why didn't you get me up for school?"

She smiled from the doorway. " I came in and called you. Twice. Kyle told me that you were having problems sleeping last night and were looking for something to help. When I went into your bathroom, I saw the Tylenol box on the counter and realized that if you'd taken one of those at the time that Kyle said, you wouldn't wake up, even for my specialty. So I called the school, and let you sleep."

"Thanks, Mom. I probably shouldn't have taken the pills last night, but I couldn't sleep. I've been so tired lately, I just wanted to check out for a bit."

She walked over, gave me a hug and bent to retrieve my pajamas form the floor. "Everyone does it once and a while. Next time please let me—Stevie, why are your pajamas wet?"

"I don't really know. I had another one of those incredibly vivid dreams again, after I took the pills. Maybe that has something to do with it?"

"I'll be glad when this whole curse thing is behind us," she said with a shrug. "I'll throw these in the wash." Another hug and then she left me to my own thoughts.

I grabbed my notebook form my bag, and started detailing this dream. Maybe the answer was embedded in there somewhere.

Trying to figure out what I was missing from my notes of my dreams was useless. My mind didn't want to, or couldn't, focus on what I'd written. The day was nearly half over, and I was still lounging around sipping my tea and staring out the window.

I texted Ian and Chrissy, apologizing to both, but neither of them texted me back. That was far more depressing than the threat from some two-hundred year old witch. I needed to find a way to get back to talking terms with my friends.

My eyes filled; I thought about what I'd had with Ian. How a simple misunderstanding had destroyed that. I felt desolate sitting there.

"Mom, I'm going to see if Emily is up to having a visitor for a little while. I don't feel like going in or being alone with myself as company."

"What's up?" she asked.

"I just started thinking about Ian. I miss him; his laugh and his company. I don't know how to make it right again." I stared out the window, "Maybe talking with a girlfriend will shed some light on things."

Fifteen minutes later, I was walking up the steps to Emily's house. It was a cute little Cape Cod house that Emily and her mom shared. The door opened as I was on the first step.

"Hey, Stranger," Emily called out.

"Oh, you're a sight for sore eyes, Emily." I chuckled and threw my arms around her.

We settled into the tiny living room, Emily sprawled on the couch and I flopped into the armchair. "How've you been feeling?" I asked.

She shrugged. "Guess I'm doing okay. The head still hurts, but we're surviving. How are you doing? Ian texted me last night."

"Oh. I'm, er, um, I don't know," I sighed. "Right now I feel like my life has been thrown into a mixer that's been set on puree."

"What happened?"

"He was upset because I was more concerned about solving the clue than running over to sit with Chrissy. Which sounds harsher than it was, but essentially, that was it."

"I heard she really had a hard time yesterday," Emily said as she looked at something through the window. "I can see how both obligations would tear at you. Did you make the right choice?"

"Em, I don't know what I'm feeling right now. Ian hasn't responded to my text or voicemail. Neither has Chrissy. I feel that I made significant progress on the clue, so I don't know."

Her eyes perked up. "Did you figure it out?" she asked sounding like a kid on Christmas.

"I broke the code. I know that the clue is about loyalty, but now I'm trying to figure out what I need to do about it."

Her phone chirped, she glanced down and frowned. Her fingers flew over the keys as she sent a quick response. "Sorry about that. It was, um, someone from school."

"Ian?" I asked quietly.

She nodded. "Yeah. The whole breaking up thing has been hard on him too. And since he sort of joined in with our group shortly after he moved here, he really doesn't have many other friends to help him with this."

I leaned forward and placed my head in my hands and rocked slowly. "This is so much harder than I thought. I was hoping that you and I could talk through this, but if you're acting as his sounding board as well, I don't want you to end up in the middle."

"It's okay, Stevie. I don't think that I'll be there long," she said with a smile. My phone vibrated in my pocket.

I glanced at the display, "Ian wants me to call him after school, so we can talk." I let out a breath that I didn't know that I'd been holding.

Emily's phone chirped again while I was texting Ian to let him know that I would call. When I was done, I looked up. Her eyes were wide and her mouth was frozen open.

"Emily?" I waved my hand in front of her and she didn't even blink. "Hey! Em!" I reached over and touched her leg. She jumped.

"Oh, God, Stevie!" Her face contorted so she looked like she was in pain.

"What is it?"

"Dee just texted me. She overheard a group of kids planning to confront Chrissy tonight."

"Blast it all, do we know when?"

"Dee said she thinks around seven."

"Where?" My mind was already engaging into security mode. If I knew when and where we could find a way to stop it.

"That's the thing. She didn't hear. She was trying to find out, but somebody noticed her, and since she hangs with us sometimes, they quieted right down."

"Why don't you forward that message on to Ian," I though for a moment and then added, "and Chrissy. Let's give everyone that is involved a heads up. Maybe we can stop this before it goes too far."

We spent the rest of the afternoon bouncing ideas off of each other. Regardless with what we came up with, Emily wasn't gong to be going far. She was still on a medical lock-down with her mother. Ian responded back to us about the warning, but there was no word from Chrissy.

I left for home around three, and figured that perhaps I could get a few hours of pondering the task that I still needed to complete. Unfortunately, I didn't get far as I fell asleep on my window bench shortly after I got in.

Something brushed my cheek, and I felt a cold wet object pressing into my eye. Opening the other one, I saw Misty had climbed up to the seat with me and was insistent to cover my entire face with kisses. "Hey, Mist. What's up?"

Her only response was a quick yip and the increased tempo of her wagging stub of a tail.

I looked out the window and noticed that it was getting dark. "What time is it?" I asked the dog, who looked at me as if I'd asked her if she wanted a treat. I glanced up to the nightstand and looked at the clock. "Oh blast! It's after six and I don't have a clue where that gang is going to go looking for Chrissy!"

Jumping to my feet, I sent the dog into bouts of barking and she was crouching down wanting to play. "Not now, Misty. We've got to find Chrissy." I ran down the stairs with her right on my heels and we skidded into the kitchen.

"Dinner will be ready in about twenty minutes, Stevie, so no snacks right now."

"Mom, can I borrow the car for a bit? I know that I'm going to miss dinner right now, but I'll get something when I get back."

"Where are you going?"

"Something's up with Chrissy, and I need to see what I can do to help."

"Is she alright?" concerned my mom set down the burgers that she was getting ready to broil.

"Not sure. I got a text that there was a rumor that a gang of kids were going to confront her tonight. But nobody is saying where. It may not happen, but I can't take that chance."

"Okay, but, Stevie, be careful."

I grabbed the car keys from the peg by the door, slipped my coat on and was about to walk out when Misty sat by the door. I clipped her leash on and we headed out. I called Ian as I walked to the car. "Hi, Ian," I said tentatively when he answered.

"Hi. I'm not going to have much time to talk right now, Stevie," he said tersely. Apparently I hadn't yet been forgiven.

"Me either, I still haven't heard back form Chrissy, so I'm taking the car and heading out. Not sure yet where I'm going to go."

"Sounds like we're all doing the same thing. I'll talk to you later."

"Listen, where are you going to cover? I don't want to waste time covering the same areas."

"Okay, that makes sense. I'm planning to head down to the docks, and check out around the train tracks."

"Okay, I'll try some areas in town."

"Stevie," he paused for a brief moment. "I'm glad that you're in on this. We have a lot to talk through."

"Yeah, we do. I'm glad I'm back too." We hung up as Misty and I climbed into the car.

I started to drive towards town, looked in at Scoops, and checked out the parking lot at school. I struck out on both counts. "Where would they go, Misty?" I asked the dog while I scratched her ears.

My mind went back to the conversation with the witch from my dream. The answer hit suddenly. "I know where they are going!" shouted and Misty barked. I grabbed my phone and texted Ian to meet us there, and sped off to the edge of town, hoping that we wouldn't be too late.

CHAPTER 24

ACTION

Racing across town was two gambles for the price of one: I could be mistaken and the mob wasn't where I thought they were, and if I saw any of the town's law enforcement officers, they could give me a ticket for speeding. I was willing to risk both.

I pulled up just outside of the woods that surround the cemetery. Either there was a late night funeral going on, or I'd hit the jackpot of where everyone else was. Now I just had to get there in time before Chrissy got hurt.

"Come on, Misty," I said giving her leash a tug. We hurried up to the front gate. I couldn't see any one there, but there was some noise that seemed to be coming from one of the back corners. I was about to step in, when someone called.

"Stevie!"

I turned and saw Ian running up the walk. "Hi. I think that they're in there. If you listen, you can hear them."

"How do you think we should handle this?"

"I was thinking that we could walk in, take a look around. If we're right, it just takes a minute of so to call the police."

He was thinking when Dee came up. "Hey, guys. Is this it?"

I looked at Ian. "I called her," he said. "There was just too much area to cover with just the two of us, and since Emily is out of commission right now, I used what resources I had available."

I turned to Dee, "It looks like this is the place. We were thinking that we would walk in and verify that this is the place. If it is, we can call for help and try to make sure that nothing happens."

"Sounds like a plan," she said. "Let's go"

The three of us made our way around the perimeter of the small cemetery, staying close to the shadows that were cast by the woods.

Misty suddenly began to pull on her leash. "Whoa, Girl," I whispered. At this point, I really wasn't ready to sound the alarm. We crept along in a single file line, with Misty out in front pulling me, Dee and then Ian in the back.

Cautiously, we made our way around the plots until we came to the back corner. There they were. It looked to be at least thirty-five people there. They were all chanting some ridiculous saying. It didn't exactly make me feel warm and fuzzy. I heard a soft moan, and I looked to the center of the mob; my heart froze.

Chrissy was tied to a tree trunk. Even from this distance, I could see that she'd already gone a round or two with someone. I stopped, turned to look at Ian and pointed. His eyes bulged when he recognized what was going on.

"They're going to kill her," Dee said holding her hand to her mouth in shock.

"We've got to do something," I said. Looking back at the horror scene that was being played out twenty yards away. My stomach tightened, and I felt like I was going to be sick.

Ian pulled out his phone, "Ah, man. Why is it when you need these things the most, it is always at the point where you don't have any service?"

Dee and I both checked our phones. "Nothing," I agreed.

"Stevie, why don't you and Dee stay here? I'll make a quick dash back and call as soon as I can get a signal. Once the cops are on the way, we can make some type of diversion."

"How," Dee asked, "is that going to help Chrissy?"

I shrugged. "Getting the cops here ASAP is the first step. The diversion will buy us time. The more time that they are delayed, the less damage that they can do to her."

With a nod, Ian slipped back into the shadows. My eyes stayed focused on the group in front of me. As an after thought, I pulled out my phone and turned on the camera function to shoot a video.

"Why are you shooting a video?"

"Well, when Chrissy was attacked, they had several leads, but as of right now, or at least last I heard, there still haven't been any arrests. Perhaps the video will be able to give the police the evidence that they need to make some."

"That makes sense, I suppose." That's when everything went down hill for us.

A twig snapped behind us which spooked Misty, who responded by barking.

A voice from the crowd surged forward, "Somebody's out there. Get 'em before they can cause us problems."

I turned to Dee and handed her my phone. "Run! They heard Misty; I'll go this way and lead them away from you. Go!"

She took my phone and looked at me with a pained expression. "You'll be caught!"

"Yep. Now go, or they'll get both of us." I gave her a little push, and she started running but continued to glance over her shoulder until she was out of sight. "Okay, Mist, let's go get caught and hope for the best."

We hadn't taken more than two steps out of the shadows before a boy yelled, "I see 'em. Over here." I stopped where I was.

Four guys circled us. I didn't recognize any of them. "Well, well, well," the biggest one said. "Looks like you picked a bad place to take a walk tonight."

Misty growled and cowered into my leg. I kept hoping that I'd hear the sounds of sirens signaling the oncoming charge of the cavalry. But all I heard was the chirps of the crickets. "Um, hi. I didn't realize that you were all here. We'll, uh, we'll just be going now," I said hopefully and tried to turn away.

A guy with very wide shoulders and a blond crew cut stood directly in my path. "I don't think you're going anywhere."

Somebody grabbed me and spun me around; there was a flash of fur a yowl of pain, and then a yip. "Hey! Don't hit my dog!"

"Then teach that mutt not to bite people."

"Perhaps if you'd leave me alone, she wouldn't feel the need to protect me."

"Enough!" a bass voice said sternly. He had to be seven feet tall, and his skin was almost as dark as the night itself. "I don't want anybody to touch the girl, or the dog, until we decide what we is going to do with them. Got it?"

Crew cut nodded and the other two mumbled what I took as their agreement. The big guy pulled my arm and led me towards the center of the group.

Reaching the main part of the mob, I had a startling revelation. It was going to be nearly impossible for me to get away, let alone help Chrissy. I thought back to the dream with the witch; she'd said that it would be over tonight. At this rate, it looked like she'd be right. Barring a miracle, I was pretty sure I was going to end up dead before the sun rose in the morning.

"We found her, and this dog, lurking over by the edge of the woods there."

A familiar voice sounded from the night. "Ah, Tanya, look. It's our old friend Stevie. Stevie Nixon, right? Never were able to keep your nose out of other people's business, were you?" Did you come here to watch us beat this worthless twit?" she asked me.

"Gabby, what's your problem?" I replied. "What's the deal here?"

"What's the deal? Oh, that's right, you like the little queer." she sneered.

"I'm just more concerned with doing what's right. This looks like a group of vigilantes or something; like, forty against a single girl," I replied.

"Oh, little goodie two shoes! Sorry. I forgot you got a thing for weirdos. Oh, no, I mean, actually, I don't really care."

I was physically dragged over to the tree where Chrissy was. Somebody took the leash from my hand and tied it to the tree.

My hands were tied together and an unseen hand forced me to the ground.

"Thevie? Fat you?" Chrissy said through a bruised and swollen mouth.

"Yeah, Chrissy, it's me. I'm sorry I wasn't there last night."

"Saw right. I fink dey're gonna kill us," Chrissy managed to choke out.

"Help is on the way," I said softly. "Ian went to call the police, so we just need to make it a little while longer." I knew that our best hope lay in trying to get them talking and give the police time to arrive.

I looked out at the assembled mob, and had a quick flashback to a scene out of Mary Shelley's novel, *Frankenstein*. All that was missing were the torches and pitchforks. But for all I knew, they could have had those in their cars.

I had to try to think of a way to change the ending so that we all came out alive and as unscathed as possible.

Where were the police? Where were Ian and Dee? Why wasn't anyone coming yet?

I took a deep breath to try and steady my nerves. I craned my neck around until I could see Misty. She seemed okay, curled up and taking a nap. Looking back at Chrissy, I said, "Chrissy, I'm going to do everything that I can to make sure that none of us die here tonight.

I turned to Tony, "So what's the big deal Tony? Are you that unnerved by someone who is not like you?"

Tony stopped his conversation with Gabby and Tanya and came over. "We just don't like people who don't follow the rules," he spat. "This is a boy, and he wants to be a girl. That ain't right!"

"So it's right for you to be judge, jury and executioner? Listen, all of you," I'd raised my voice and now the mumbling stopped. All eyes were on me. "What reason do you have for doing this to her? Because she's different? Well, news flash. We're all different. Each of us has a unique personality and tastes that makes us who we are."

I looked over at the tall guy, "It wasn't that long ago that we had people killing each other over the color of our skin. But does the color of your skin make any difference? We're all human beings; we all deserve to be able to live our lives."

"Yeah," the tall guy yelled back. "But we didn't have any choice of what color we were."

"Do you really think she has a choice? Many of you heard Mrs. Lerch at the assembly the other day. This is the result of a medical condition. The doctor who was there said the same thing. Nobody would ever choose to go through this. They go through it because it is the only way that they can live.

"And you all decide that because it's not you, or one of your friends, that someone who has already suffered for years with this shouldn't be allowed to exist because they've decided to be authentic? What does that make you? You're upset because she doesn't fit your definition of male or female. But if you hurt her, do you think you should even qualify as human."

I looked around the group. It appeared as though the immediate intent to kill us had dissipated, for now at least.

"Chrissy found the courage to be who she is; so she could look in the mirror and be proud of the image that faced back at her. How will you look at the image in the mirror if you follow through on this? How will you look when you have blood on your hands?"

The crowd was still silent, but my ears were echoing with the sounds of my own heartbeat. In the distance, a siren wailed and drew nearer. I'd run out of things to say, so I had to hope that they would think for a few minutes before they acted. At least give the emergency crews time to get here.

"Stevie's right." I looked towards the voice and was shocked that it was Gabby that spoke. "We all want to be accepted for who we are, yet when one of our classmates doesn't conform, we want to act destructively." She walked over to me, and released my hands. "I'm sorry about this, Stevie." Together, we freed Chrissy. "I hope that you both will accept my apologies for my behaviors."

She started to walk away, and I was torn; part of me wanted her to pay for what she had done, but part wondered if she had come to her senses. I was stunned when she sat on one of the headstones, and waited for the police to make their way to the group.

As Chrissy was loaded onto a gurney, Misty tangled her leash around my legs and I relaxed for the first time in nearly three months. I looked around the cemetery; Ian and Dee were talking to one officer, Gabby was talking to Officer Addams. Sheriff Guliano was walking towards me.

"Impressive speech there, Ms. Nixon."

I cocked my head, "How do you know?"

"Your friend, Dee, recorded the whole thing on your cell phone. It's gong to make things a lot easier down the road. Turns out that the three boys we were planning to arrest in the morning for the attack at the school were here tonight as well. So, we've served them a warrant, and they'll be arraigned in the morning."

"What about everyone else?"

"Well, the video doesn't show everyone else, but there are a few that we will be talking to. And to be honest, I'm kind of impressed with the young lady over on the stone there," he pointed to Gabby. "She came up to me, and admitted her whole part in this. She's taking responsibility for her own actions and has agreed to give us names of who else was involved tonight."

"I'm surprised, but glad."

"You did a fine job. I'll be talking to you tomorrow. Have a good night."

I walked over to where Dee and Ian were now waiting. "We did it."

Ian pulled me in and gave me a hug. "Yeah, we did, Stevie. I'm proud of you."

"Let's head over to the hospital to be there for Chrissy."

CHAPTER 25:

FRIENDSHIP

Feeling refreshed when I woke in the mornings was something that I had forgotten over the past months, so I was surprised when it happened this morning. No disturbing dreams, nothing that appeared out of the ordinary. The only reason that I could think of for this marvelous event was that it was over. Okay, this part of the curse was over.

I stretched while lying in bed, and Misty seemed to sense that I was awake. She did her own stretch and then padded up to lick my face. "Hey, Pup," I said while I scratched her ears.

I lay there just enjoying the peace that I felt. Chrissy had been treated and released last night. She was going to be sore, for sure, but that was minor when you considered what might have happened if things hadn't been stopped.

There was a knock on my door, and it slowly opened, "Stevie? Are you up?" Mom asked.

"Yeah. It feels good this morning."

"I spoke to Joyce last night. She told me what you did at the cemetery. I'm very proud of you." She leaned over and hugged me.

"I just did what was right."

"Not everyone would have been as brave as you were. Always remember, regardless of what happens, I love you." She added a kiss and then headed downstairs to get breakfast going.

Downstairs, I found Kyle and my dad laughing. "You look pretty chipper this morning," Dad said.

"I feel pretty good. It seems that the big worries for this round are behind me now. That lets me relax, even if it's only for a day or so, but it sure feels good."

Kyle paused with a forkful of French toast almost to his mouth and looked at me. "Do you really think it's over for now?"

"When I got home last night, I pulled out the original clue, and went over it again. Combined with what I had in my notebook, as far as I can tell, it is. It feels like it is. The clue was the word loyalty; the medal that I found had the same word along with symbols that were used to represent loyalty two hundred years ago. These same symbols were on Ichabod Crane's gravestone. It adds up for me."

Everyone was quiet for a few minutes as we ate; each of lost in our own thoughts.

I got a ride to school from Dad, which meant that I got there earlier than normal. But this was fine with me. After getting things cleared with the main office, I spent half an hour hanging signs around the school, asking students to attend the first meeting of Sleepy Hollow High's Gay-Straight-Trans Alliance. I was hanging the last sign when Emily found me.

"Always busy? Huh?"

"Emily! It's so good to see you back at school. How are you feeling?"

"I've been better, but the headaches have pretty much subsided, so I'm ready to take it on and go for it."

I dropped the tape and hugged her tightly. "I've missed you around here."

"From what I've heard, you've really stepped up to the plate and hit the homerun to win the game." When I looked at her with a puzzled look, she laughed, "Chrissy called me."

"When? She didn't get out of the hospital until after midnight last night."

"She called me this morning. She should be here anytime."

Just as she said this, I heard clapping. I turned in the direction that it came from, and my throat grew tight. Our classmates were clapping for Chrissy as she hobbled down the hall. Perhaps there was hope after all for things to work out.

Accepting each other was what I was now campaigning for. I was hoping that after last night's show down, we had at least turned the corner. Each of us had to try to stand for what was right, and do our best to support our friends.

I'd finally figured this out last night when I'd made my stand for Chrissy. I realized then that I may not win, but at least I would have a clear conscience.

The group of students had made its way down to where Emily and I were standing. Chrissy threw her arms around us. "Thank you, both of you. What I've had to go through these last few weeks would have been impossible if it wasn't for you girls and Ian."

I felt the pats of hands on my back from my classmates, as the comments of 'way to go" and "great job" were bantered about with "you showed true courage". I tried to be modest, but it was hard when there were literally fifty people wanting to congratulate me.

Getting through the day was a fairly easy prospect. People were happy that things seemed to work out for the best. I noticed that a few people weren't in attendance today, most notably Tony, Tanya and Gabby.

At three-o-clock, we met in Mrs. Vallente's room. I couldn't believe my eyes: I was hoping that we would have a few people in attendance, but I wasn't expecting the seventy-five that showed up. Another positive sign that we were making progress.

As we were leaving the school we headed towards Ian's car. We had decided that after last night, we wanted something more than ice cream. After a quick debate it was decided that it had to be pizza. As we approached the car, I saw a figure sitting on the hood, and my fist unconsciously balled. Before I could say anything, Ian's cousin stood up and put her hands in the air.

"Truce?" Gabby asked tentatively.

"What do you want, Gabby?" Ian demanded.

"Look, I screwed up, okay. Chris—sy I need to apologize to you. You've shown strength and poise over the last few weeks, and those of us who gave you a hard time were jealous that you could handle something like this as well as you did. That undermines people like Tony and he feels threatened. And truthfully, I acted like a jerk as well, simply because I've made my reputation by putting others down.

"I just wanted to tell you, that I admitted everything that I did last night, and the other times, when I was at the sheriff's office last night. This morning at the arraignment, I was the only one who pled guilty. I know that what I did was wrong, and, Stevie, what you said last night hit home . I need to be able to look at myself in the mirror, and it was getting harder each day. I'll accept what ever the court decides is my punishment, and I'm going to try to pick up the pieces of my life and learn from these mistakes."

"I'm surprised with you, Gabby," Ian said. "What happens next?"

She shrugged her shoulders. "I'm not sure, honestly. I'm trying to figure out how I'm going to graduate from here, while I'm incarcerated."

"Do you think that you'll have to do jail time?" Emily asked, sincerely worried.

"Nobody really knows. The sheriff says that because I was willing to help out in the aftermath, that they may go easy and I'll only get probation. But if that's not the case, I'm going to do what's right. I'm not sure what will happen to the others. Right now no one else is talking to me. They all figure I'm a fink because I ratted them out. Anyway, I wanted to let you know, and extend my apologies." She turned to walk away.

Chrissy surprised me. She hobbled quickly and caught up with Gabby. She touched her shoulder and then gave her a hug. "Listen," she said, "we're all going out for a pizza. Do you want to join us?"

Gabby looked at the group of us. "I'm not sure, I'm—"

"Come on, Gabby," I said. "You look like you could use some company right now."

I'm not sure who was more shocked: her or Ian. She looked at me with wide eyes, and then nodded her head, "Okay, yeah I'd love to come. I'll even buy."

With that, we all piled into the car and headed for Donetello's Pizzeria.

That night as I got ready for bed, I relayed how things had gone to my mom. She was as shocked as I was about Gabby's turn around. "I'm glad," I said, "that she seems to be doing the right thing right now, but I wonder how long it's going to last?"

"Well, I guess we'll just have to see. It sounds like something that you said triggered this response. Perhaps she is just finally growing up." Mom got up and walked over to where I was brushing my hair. Taking the brush, she continued brushing and finally asked me, "How are you feeling tonight? I mean, it's the eve of the equinox."

I saw her hand tremble slightly, "Mom, It's going to be fine. I'm relaxed and at peace with myself. I'm certain that this part of the curse has been fulfilled. It means that I've got one more section to go, and then I will have broken it for all of our future generations."

"I'm glad that you feel that way. I'll be nervous for both of us, okay?" she chuckled.

I tried to laugh, but it was hard thinking about what she was worried about. "Mom, listen everything is going to be fine. I've got a great family and friends that have helped me through this. We deciphered the clue and, when it was tested, my loyalty proved rock solid. I beat this one, I can feel it."

She kissed my forehead, "Okay, then. Get some sleep, and we'll see you in the morning."

I crawled into bed, Misty snuggled up next to me and I ran though everything in my head. There was nothing else I could do, but believe that I would wake in the morning.

Yawning I blinked in the sunlight that was now streaming through my window. Misty stretched and yawned before she padded up to get her ritual morning scratch. I looked over at the desk, and saw the box.

I wasn't really raring to get into this one; it was the last and I had to assume the most challenging of the three tasks. But it was the last; I'd made it to the final task.

I walked slowly to my desk, took a deep breath and lifted the cover. And shrieked, "Are you kidding me!"

Well at least we've got three months to figure this one out.

KEEP READING FOR A SPECIAL PREVIEW

OF THE NEXT BOOK

IN THE **SLEEPY HOLLOW HIGH** SERIES

SAVAGE SPRING

COMING MARCH 20, 2014

Seeing the sun this morning was verification that I had completed the task for the last clue, loyalty, within the time constraint. I had completed the first two, now I had to get ready to face the third and final challenge. I looked over to my desk, and even in the early morning dawn, I could make out the thin black box that would hold the clue that would explain what needed to be done to finally, and forever, break this curse.

My white and buff cocker spaniel, Misty, stretched and plodded her way up the bed to poke at me with her nose. "Hey, Girl. We made it. This is the last one." I slid out of bed and shuffled over to the inconspicuous box and took a couple of deep breaths.

After seeing the first two clues, I knew that this was kind of like that gift from that elderly relation. Not quite sure what it was, but you most likely weren't going to like it. The first clue had to be translated from Latin, and then had to be recognized as being an acrostic poem. It seemed like a lot to go through to learn that you had to be honest with everyone in your life, including yourself.

Clue number two at first glance looked a bit easier. It was a series of what looked like hieroglyphics. In actuality, it was a single word written all in Greek letters. When I decoded this one, I was left with a word that was in a language that I'd never seen before. It was only through looking at the history of the town that I stumbled upon the idea that it was most likely in Dutch, and the solution to the second clue.

So, standing over the box this morning was nerve wracking to say the least. I figured that since this was it, the last challenge, the clue was going to be the hardest to solve and the resulting task would most likely test my endurance. "Here we go, Misty," I said to the dog that was still sitting on the bed watching me with her head tipped to one side.

I lifted the cover of the box, keeping my eyes nearly closed. I peeked into the box and shrieked, "Are you kidding me?"

Standing over the innocent looking box I peered down and looked at what appeared to be confetti. Upon closer inspection, I noticed that each piece was shaped differently, so this clue really was a puzzle then. "Well, that's just terrific," I snorted.

My mom, Sandy, came to the door. She is a lovely woman, petite at just five-four, slim but with generous curves. She has ash blonde hair that hangs straight and reaches to her mid back, and her eyes are a rich blue. "What's wrong, Stevie?"

Carefully, I reached into the box and grabbed a handful of the confetti, "This," I said as I poured the confetti back into the box, "is my clue."

"Oh. Well, we'll figure it out."

"That's easy for you to say, Mom. We both know how bad I am with jigsaw puzzles."

She crossed to me. "Honey, you're right. You're terrible with jigsaws, but does that mean that no one else can help you?" When I shook my head she smiled, "I on the other hand happen to love puzzles. Maybe we can work on it together." She left me to finish getting ready for school.

Knowing that doing anything useful about the clue right now was totally impracticable and otherwise impossible, I determined that I would carefully put it back in the box and not worry about it until I got home. That would give me a full six to seven hours to prepare for attempting to do a jigsaw puzzle. Who knew, maybe I'd get lucky and I'd suddenly learn how to do one while I was in Calculus class.

I placed the cover back on the box and set it into an empty desk drawer. The last thing I needed with this right now was to have the box upended and spill all of those little pieces all over the floor. And since I knew that the moment I left the house, Misty would race up the stairs and jump into the window seat to watch me leave, I knew that the odds were definitely not in my favor that the box would remain on the desk. I was better off putting it in.

Grabbing my backpack, I stuffed all of my books into it and threw in an extra sweater. It was springtime in New York, but the reality was the school's heat system didn't work the same everywhere, and some rooms were just plain colder than others.

Mom called from down stairs to let me know that breakfast was ready, so I slung my purse and backpack over my shoulder, whistled for misty and headed down. As I neared the bottom step, the smell of fresh baked coffee cake caught my attention.

I'm not sure how mom does it all. She gets up every morning and makes breakfast, and I don't just mean like cereal or something. French toast, waffles, coffee cake, these are just some of the things that she makes every morning. Then once we leave, she makes sure that the house is straightened before she locks herself into her office on the second floor where she is a freelance writer.

When Kyle and I come in from school in the afternoon, it seems that cookies have magically appeared for us, and often times they are still hot.

I followed my nose to the kitchen, where Kyle was already sitting on one of the stools stuffing a piece of steaming pastry into his mouth. "Hey, glad to see ya, Sis," he said through a mouthful of cake.

Kyle was everything that I wasn't. He was good at sports, popular with most of his classmates and he had the looks of a young god. He shared the coloring of my mom and was tall like my dad. "Good to see you too," I quipped.

He just smiled as he grabbed another piece of cake and kept eating. My dad came through the door and began to fill his own plate. My dad was an architect, who owned his own business. This meant that while he did have an office in Tarrytown, he also kept one here at home. Often he would work three days from here, and only go into the office for meetings. Today was one of those days where he was going in. He stood there in his dark pleated pants and had a cloth napkin tucked into his neckline in an effort to protect the white shirt and tie that he was wearing.

"Heard that this last clue is going to be fun, eh?"

I just glared at him. Mom had evidently told him of the confetti, and he knew just how much I loved puzzles like this.

"Stevie, look at it this way. It's no different than working on that plane that Poppy got you. You just find the right piece and put it into the correct place."

"Yeah," I said, "except there I have a copy of the plans which tells me the size the shape and any other pertinent data I need. This clue didn't even come with a picture!"

Keeping his mouth in a tight grin, Dad just nodded and took his cake with him as he headed down the hall to his office. I looked over at Kyle, who had been relatively quiet. "Do you have something to add?"

"Nope. Just glad that you made it through that part. This is it, right? This last clue is the last part of the quest. When you solve it, the curse is broken, forever. Right?"

I shrugged. "Actually, Kyle, I don't really know. As far as I know, the answer is yes. But, if you had asked me six months ago if I would have believed in any of this, I would have said no. Now it just is."

"You're going to be the one who breaks this, I know it, Stevie." He stood up and gave me a hug before he left the room. This left me stunned; I can count the number of times that Kyle has voluntarily hugged me since we became teens on one hand and have fingers left over, and my mom was standing in the corner leaning against the stove with tears streaming down her face.

"Mom? What is it?"

She shook her head and crossed to me and gave me a hug. "He is so worried about you, but doesn't know exactly how to show it."

Finishing my cake in silence, I went to get my backpack. I stood there in the hall just pondering the things that had been going on in my life. The whole idea of witches and curses still seemed too far-fetched for me, but what was I going to do? I slipped my coat on and was about ready to leave when Mom came into the back hall. "I thought you might like some brownies for your lunch today, and I'd forgotten to put them in your bag."

"Uh, thanks." I took the package, and could tell that they were still hot. "Mom, what time did you get up this morning? We had coffee cake for breakfast, and these are fresh this morning too."

Tears welled up in her eyes. "Oh, Stevie. I've just been so worried about you that I didn't sleep much last night. And it's not exactly a surprise that when I'm stressed I bake. That's what I did. I made the brownies around six this morning, with the coffee cake right after. Of course, I didn't tell anyone about the kiss cookies that will be waiting this afternoon."

She knew that these were my favorites, and I could only guess that she was making them for me today, but only after she'd been able to ensure that I was still around.

Emily was waiting for me at the edge of the driveway. I was still trying to get things back on an all-around even keel with everyone. The last task had stressed every relationship that I cherished: Emily and I didn't speak for almost a week, Ian and I broke up and Chrissy and I had shouted at each other. So, I was still apprehensive about everything.

"Hey!" Emily said with a big smile. "You're looking good on this first day of spring."

"Feeling pretty good too, Emily. Had coffee cake this morning for breakfast. Got warm brownies packed in my lunch and the promise of kiss cookies waiting for me when I get home, not too bad, eh?"

"Have you got the last clue yet?"

"Yeah," I hesitated.

"Okay. This ought to be good. What does it look like this time?"

"It looks like confetti. My mom came in right after I opened it, and she said it looked like it could be a jigsaw puzzle."

"Ooh, you don't do well with jigsaws." She slapped my arm, "Don't worry, we'll get you through it."

"Thanks," I said as we made our way to the stop.

Walking up to the crowd that was around the stop had always been kind of stressful. These were supposed to be my peers, but they often times acted like I was some kind of leper, and never talked to Emily or I. Today I was even more apprehensive than normal since when I solved the last clue; several of the very popular kids in the school had ended up being escorted to the police station.

Rumors had been flying yesterday about who was going to be getting sent away and every possible combination that could be imagined of how things had happened. The reality was, that I'd basically stopped a mob from attacking my friend Chrissy, who had just openly come out as being transgendered.

It seemed that my problems stemmed from Tony Despenzo being arrested and held in the county lockup until bail was met. Right now, everyone seemed to blame me for this. But there again, it wasn't me that caused this. To begin with, the real blame lay at Tony's feet: he's the one who led several other boys to attack Chris in the boys locker room before gym class one day. It was that attack that pushed Chris to openly admit that he'd always believed that he should be Chrissy. The change had been a bit hard on every one, but most of us were working through it.

The second attack had occurred over in the cemetery just two nights before. And the only thing that I'd done was to be loyal to my friend, and stand up for her, the day after Ian and I had broken up. But Ian had come when I called to be there for Chrissy. Ian was the one who had called the police, and it was my arch-nemesis and Ian's cousin, Gabby, who had turned evidence on the rest of those that were involved.

I thought about this as we climbed on the bus that was five minutes late, again. Ian and I had ended up working together to save Chrissy, because we shared the common goal, but we really hadn't talked much since then. We both agreed that we needed to talk, but timing just hadn't worked out.

I had wondered if Gabby had turned evidence in an attempt to get a lighter sentence. From what I had pieced together it didn't seem that she had. She'd given a complete statement in the presence of her public defender and had plead guilty before the PD had gone to the DA to try to work out a deal.

As the bus chugged along Webber Avenue on the way to the school, I wondered if she really had turned a new leaf so to speak, or if it was only for show until things were fixed. It had been nice yesterday, when she came to apologize to Chrissy and then had joined us, at Chrissy invitation, to go out for a pizza. It would be really nice if we were finally beyond the petty arguments that she and I had had since we had been in pre-K together.

About Christine...

Christine Chianti was born and raised in Western New York, where she still resides today with her family. She spent 19 years teaching high school science in a near-by city.

She is a member of the Write Touch Writing Group, Sisters in Crime, Romance Writers of America and Mystery Writers of America.

* * *

Connect with Christine:

www.christinechianti.com

www.twitter.com/cchianti

www.facebook.com/christinechianti

www.ingramcontent.com/pod-product-compliance
Lightning Source LLC
Chambersburg PA
CBHW070917260626
47162CB00007B/2701